THE HOWLING BEAST

LA BÊTE HURLANTE

THE HOWLING BEAST

By Noel Vindry

Translated by John Pugmire

The Howling Beast

First published in 1934 as *La Bête hurlante*
© *Editions GALLIMARD, Paris, 1934*

For information, contact: pugmire1@yahoo.com

FIRST AMERICAN EDITION
Library of Congress Cataloging-in-Publication Data
Vindry, Noel
[La Bête hurlante, English]
The Howling Beast / Noel Vindry
Translated from the French by John Pugmire

Introduction

Noel Vindry and the Puzzle Novel

Noel Vindry (1896-1954), wrote twelve locked room novels between 1932 and 1937, of a quality and quantity to rival his contemporary, John Dickson Carr (1905-1977), the American writer generally acknowledged to be the master of the sub-genre. Yet today Vindry remains largely forgotten by the French-speaking world and almost completely unknown in the English-speaking.

I first learned about Noel Vindry from Roland Lacourbe, the noted French locked room expert and anthologist, who calls him "the French John Dickson Carr." Much of what follows is taken from *Enigmatika No. 39: Noel Vindry,* a private publication edited by Jacques Baudou, Roland Lacourbe and Michel Lebrun, with a contribution from the author's son, Georges Vindry.

Noel Vindry came from an old Lyon family from whom he inherited his passion for culture and gourmet cuisine. Shortly after acquiring a Bachelor of Philosophy degree, he enlisted in the army, where he fought with distinction, earning a *Croix de Guerre,* but was invalided out in 1915 with severe lung damage.

During his long convalescence he studied and mastered law sufficiently to become a deputy *juge d'instruction* (examining magistrate)—a position unique to countries practising the Napoleonic Code, under which a single jurist is given total authority over a case, from investigating crime scenes to questioning witnesses; from ordering the arrest of suspects to preparing the prosecution's case, if any (see Appendix 1.)

He was appointed to serve in Aix-en-Provence in the south of France which, at the time, boasted the second largest Appeals Court outside of Paris, and which he chose because of its climate. Known as the "city of a thousand fountains," it holds a music festival every year to rival those of Bayreuth, Glyndebourne and Salzburg. In Vindry's time, it was known as *La Belle Dormante (Sleeping Beauty)* because

5

"at night you can hear the grass growing in the streets," according to Georges Vindry.

His first novel, *La Maison Qui Tue (The House That Kills)*, appeared in 1932, the same year as Carr's fourth, *The Waxworks Murder*. Both books featured detectives who were *juges d'instruction:* Vindry's Monsieur Allou and Carr's Henri Bencolin. Vindry's narrator, Lugrin, is the same age as his creator when he entered chambers, but there are few other autobiographical touches.

Vindry's book and the others that swiftly followed attracted considerable interest and, by the mid-1930s, he was one of the three most successful mystery writers in the French-speaking world, along with the two Belgian authors Georges Simenon and Stanislas-Andre Steeman. He is the only one of the three not to have had any of his books translated into English, until LRI's *The House That Kills* (2015), or brought to the screen.

In France, Vindry was hailed as the undisputed master of the "puzzle novel *(roman probleme*),"* a term he himself coined. In an essay on the detective novel written in 1933, he distinguished between the adventure novel**; the police novel; and the puzzle novel. The first deals with the acts of the criminal; the second with the capture of the criminal; and the third with the unmasking of the criminal. He held that the puzzle novel should be constructed like a mathematical problem: at a certain point, which is emphasised, all the clues will have been provided fairly, and the rigorous solution will become evident to the astute reader.

Allou himself is a deliberately dry figure about whom we learn very little. The plot and the puzzle are everything. Descriptive passages, even of entire countrysides, are kept to a minimum, as are any revelations in the narrative about characters' feelings: the omnipresent dialogue allows people to define themselves, providing ample opportunity for deception.

Already by 1934 there were rumblings from French critics that the puzzle novel, as so consummately practiced by Noel Vindry, failed to give full rein to character development.

*I prefer "puzzle novel" to "problem novel" which I feel is too ambiguous

**the detective/criminal adventure in the manner of Edgar Wallace's *The Four Just Men* and 174 other novels.

In vain had Vindry pointed out in his essay the previous year that: "The detective novel, as opposed to the psychological one, does not see the interior but only the exterior. 'States of mind' are prohibited, because the culprit must remain hidden." Nevertheless, the prominent critic Robert Brasillach asserted in *Marianne* (April, 1934) that the reign of the puzzle novel was already over and there were no more tricks left with which to bamboozle the jaded reader! (For the record, this was before Carr's *The Hollow Man* in 1935; Carter Dickson's *The Judas Window* and Clayton Rawson's *Death from a Top Hat* in 1938; and Pierre Boileau's *Six Crimes Sans Assassin,* with its six impossible murders, in 1939.) It was time to embrace crime novels rich in characterisation and atmosphere —such as those written by one M. Georges Simenon, for example.

Simenon, as is well-known, disdained the puzzle novel (despite having written several good puzzle short stories in his early career as Georges Sim) because he saw it as too rigid and too much under the influence of Anglo-Saxon writers. In his novels, the plot and the puzzle—if there is one—are a distant second to atmosphere and the psychology of the characters: the complete antithesis of Vindry's works. And, to further distance himself from the classical detective fiction of the period, it is the humble policeman and not the gifted amateur or the high functionary who solves the case. Thus were the seeds of the police procedural planted at the very peak of the Golden Age.

From 1932 to 1937 both Simenon and Vindry wrote at the same frantic rate as John Dickson Carr/Carter Dickson. After that, Vindry wrote only one more puzzle novel before World War II. Even though he announced on a Radio Francaise broadcast in 1941 that he was abandoning detective fiction because it didn't amuse him any more, he nevertheless wrote three more shortly before he died in 1954; none of them featured M. Allou and, after such a long break from his earlier success, his books failed to sell well.

By this time, however, his views had mellowed and he had become more accommodating towards the detective novel, which he defined, in a 1953 letter to the editor of *Mystère-Magazine* (see Appendix 2), as "a mystery drama emphasizing logic," and consisting of three elements:

1. A drama, the part with the action
2. A mystery, the poetic part
3. The logic, the intelligent part

"They are terribly difficult to keep in equilibrium. If drama dominates, we fall into melodrama or worse, as everyone knows; if mystery dominates, we finish up with a fairy tale, something altogether different which doesn't obey the same laws of credibility; if logic dominates, the work degenerates into a game, a chess problem or a crossword and it's no longer a novel."

A great example of equilibrium? Gaston Leroux's *Le Mystere de la Chambre Jaune (The Mystery of the Yellow Room)* published in 1908. This, of course, was also declared by Carr to be the greatest locked room mystery of all.

Meanwhile, Simenon powered on and was next rivalled by Boileau-Narcejac. Pierre Boileau and Thomas Narcejac, individually successful as puzzle novel writers, teamed up following an award dinner for Narcejac to which Boileau, as a previous winner, had been invited. Their novels, while maintaining the brilliant puzzle plots dreamt up by Boileau, relaxed the rigid puzzle novel formula espoused by Vindry and incorporated Narcejac's descriptive and character work.

Although he may have been a shooting star, Noel Vindry was much admired by his peers. Steeman, in a letter to Albert Pigasse, the founder of *Le Masque,* in 1953, suggested that, even though Vindry's latest work was his weakest, he deserved a prize which everyone—readers and critics alike—would realise was for the ensemble of his work. Narcejac, writing in *Combat* after Vindry's death in 1954, asserted that nobody, not even "those specialists E. Queen and D. Carr" *(sic),* was the equal of the master, Noel Vindry. Even though the puzzle-novel was well and truly dead, if he had to designate its poet, he would not hesitate: it would be Vindry. And, in their 1964 memoir on *Le Roman Policier* (The Detective Novel), Boileau and Narcejac spoke of his "unequalled virtuosity" and "stupefying puzzles."

If Golden Age Detection needed a patron saint, then Noel Vindry would surely be a candidate.

John Pugmire

CHAPTER I

THE STRANGE ENCOUNTER

M. Allou, with his customary smooth stride, was walking briskly in the vicinity of the Gare Saint-Lazare. Not because he was in a hurry, but because in Paris in late March there were often sudden wintry spells. In fact, everyone else was doing the same.

Despite the crisp cold reddening his cheeks, there was a happy smile on his thin face. It was the start of his Paris vacation.

The previous day, he had spent the entire afternoon in his chambers in the Marseille Palais de Justice, sorting out the voluminous dockets he was trying to leave in good order for the colleague who would replace him. And now, after the overnight journey, he could sense all around him the intelligence and finesse of the capital city and think, in eager anticipation, of nights in the theatre, concerts and art exhibitions, notably the Cezanne retrospective he'd read about on the train.

But, at that particular moment, it was the thought of a more immediate and more material pleasure which was bringing the smile to his lips. The clock had just struck twelve and he was about to enjoy one of those succulent lunches he treated himself to every day. Amongst his friends, his gourmandise was admired even more than his marvellous perspicacity—and he himself attached more importance to his gourmet tastes than to his powers of deduction.

Thus it was that, preoccupied with thoughts of the meal ahead, he was paying little attention to the passers-by. Just as he was passing in front of the Gare Saint-Lazare, however, a man leaning motionless against the railings drew his attention.

He was tall, with a bony, tanned face and a broken nose. He, too, having seemingly ignored everyone else, shot a look at M. Allou. His attention had undoubtedly been caught by the latter's strange blue eyes, so thoughtful yet so determined, which those he interrogated never forgot.

The magistrate kept on walking, although the two men continued to eye each other. As M. Allou drew level with the other, he turned his

9

head to look straight at him.

The man took two steps forward and they stared directly at each other.

'I haven't eaten for three days, monsieur,' said the man in a low voice.

There was no trace of any humility. His clothes, for that matter, were not those of a beggar; quite the opposite, they were of a sober elegance, except for—and this was quite startling—a crumpled collar.

M. Allou was quite sure the man wasn't lying. It was enough to look at his dark, hollow eyes, too brilliant and too feverish. They were the eyes of a hungry wolf...and even a hunted one.

'Come with me,' said the magistrate, simply.

The man followed him silently to a nearby restaurant. On seeing it was crowded, M. Allou changed his mind and chose a smaller one, where they ensconced themselves in a corner.

'Would you mind,' asked the man, 'if I kept my hat on?'

It was jammed down over his eyes, as M. Allou had noted earlier, subconsciously, in the street.

'Just as you wish,' he replied.

'I should explain. It's because—.'

'No explanation necessary. Allow me to introduce myself. I'm M. Allou, examining magistrate.'

The unknown other went suddenly pale. He pushed down on the table with clenched hands as if he were going to make a run for it. He seemed to change his mind, hesitated, then took off his hat.

'Look at me,' he said.

The magistrate looked up briefly, then returned to the menu. The man seemed to lose patience.

'So, go ahead and arrest me!' he said in a subdued voice. 'I've had enough. Enough! I prefer to get it over with, do you hear! Let me eat, then arrest me!'

M. Allou gave him a cold, hard look. He waited for the waiter to place two plates of hors-d'oeuvre on the table, then pushed one towards the other man.

'Eat up,' he said. 'As for arresting you, I'm outside my area of authority. And, besides, I don't know who you are.'

The man said nothing for several minutes, wolfing the food down almost without chewing, then looked at M. Allou again.

'Can't you see the scar?' he asked brusquely.

'Yes, I noticed it.'

He would have been hard put not to see it. It was a red gash, made recently, which extended across the forehead. The skin had not yet healed, so the flesh beneath was clearly visible.

'So, can't you guess?'

'No.'

'But I've an easily recognisable face.'

'I don't know anything.'

'Don't you read the newspapers?'

'Rarely, and I only skim them.'

The man pulled a news cutting out of his pocket and offered it to M. Allou. He pointed to a photograph of himself under a headline: *"Pierre Herry On The Run."*

'Now do you recognise me? I'm Pierre Herry!'

The magistrate looked at the headlines at the top of the page, which read, in large thick letters:

"THE DOUBLE MURDER OF CHATEAU DE SAINT-LUCE. PIERRE HERRY, THE KILLER, STILL ON THE RUN"

The same headline had been in the newspapers for several days. M. Allou had noticed it, but had not read any further. News articles rarely interested him and, besides, there was no mystery: the murderer's name had been known from the beginning.

'I'm Pierre Herry,' the man repeated in the same subdued voice.

'For now, you're my guest and nothing more,' replied M.Allou. 'You confided in me spontaneously and I haven't the right to betray you. When you're no longer hungry, you can leave and I'll forget we ever met.'

'No, I prefer to be arrested. I've had enough.'

He spoke so wearily that M. Allou was struck by the contrast with the energy in his face. Was he overwhelmed by remorse? It didn't seem so.

'I've had enough,' he repeated. 'The hunger's unbearable. I've not had a *sou* in my pocket for three days and haven't dared to steal or even beg... Why did I approach you? I've no idea. It was the way you looked at me, I think, which decided me. I felt that any request I

11

made wouldn't demean me. You're allowed to beg if you're really hungry, don't you think?

'And the worst of it wasn't even the hunger. Nor was it being hunted like a beast. Nor having to turn my head and lose myself in the crowd whenever anyone looked at me—I don't like running away, I can assure you. No, the worst of all....'

He became agitated as he spoke and his eyes gleamed intensely. Was it just because he had finally eaten something, the stimulation not just of the wine but of the food as well? M. Allou thought so for a moment, but was soon set straight, because the fugitive continued, in a low but passionate voice:

'No, the worst of all is the silence! Needing to confide, needing to know whether one is going mad or not, whether one's reasoning is normal. That, you cannot imagine. I was in need of a confidant, monsieur, even more than a meal. If I'm mad, then please tell me, for pity's sake. I prefer to know, rather than wallow in this uncertainty!'

He was speaking more loudly now, but luckily the room was empty. Nevertheless, M. Allou touched him lightly on the arm to calm him down and said:

'I didn't ask you to confide in me. Don't forget that, if I'm called to testify, I shall be obliged to repeat everything.'

'I don't care. I don't want to hide the truth, as least as it appears to me. You shall know what I saw, or thought I saw. And I'll repeat it when they arrest me.'

'Are you guilty or innocent?' asked M. Allou.

'I don't know. Logically, I should be guilty. No reasonable man would claim otherwise. My reason, for what it's worth, tells me I must be a criminal. And yet I believe myself to be innocent.'

M. Allou stared hard at him, wondering whether he was being tricked. Was Pierre Herry simply pretending to be mad, in order for the magistrate to attest to that later?

He said nothing and concentrated on filling his pipe.

He'd already had experiences with tricksters in the past, and discovered there was only one way to catch them out: oblige them to describe everything in minute detail, when they would inevitably betray themselves.

He looked up.

'I'll listen,' he said, 'because you want to talk. But I don't know anything about the case. You'll have to tell me everything in detail.'

Pierre Herry took a surprisingly large bundle of cuttings out of his pocket and placed it on the table.

'Read these,' he replied.

'No, that would take too long. I can use them as needed whilst you tell your story. You can start now.'

The other seemed distressed. He took his head in his hands, remained silent for a long time, and finally murmured:

'Where to start? Does it all go back a long way, or are the last few days separate from the rest? And what's important?'

'Everything, for the moment. Don't omit the slightest detail. Now, calm down. What are the facts?'

Pierre Herry picked up the pile of cuttings and searched through them with an unsteady hand.

CHAPTER II

LE COMTE DE SAINT-LUCE

'Here, look at this photograph. Saint-Luce's castle, ten kilometres from Versailles. Can you imagine such a sinister place, less than thirty kilometres from Paris?

'Beyond the trees lining the walls of the castle park, you can just make out a vast stretch of moorland reaching as far as the horizon. You can't imagine how barren and desolate it is. Nothing grows there except a few thin shrubs and the only creatures are sheep.'

'I can see that. But the park looks leafy.'

'True, but that doesn't make it any more cheerful. The vegetation there, in contrast with the moor, is excessively luxuriant. It gets dark there even before the sun goes down. And there are no vistas anywhere.'

'And around the edges?'

'The park is enclosed by a wall three metres high, just like a prison! And there are no gaps other than a single iron gate, which is so old and rusty you can hardly open it. It has a small door cut into it which can be bolted. It's the only place from which you can see the surrounding countryside, miserable as it is. There, you can see it on the photograph.'

'A miserable spot, indeed,' said M. Allou. 'I wouldn't have built a castle there.'

'In the olden days they didn't worry about the landscape. They probably built it there because there was water, which would enable them to resist a siege.'

'It's not very clear from the photograph. Is the castle really as old as it appears?'

'Some parts were restored at the beginning of the last century—the tower on the right, notably. But most of it dates from the fourteenth century. It's riddled with interior courtyards, some narrow, some deep, and I haven't even seen half of them. Here you can see a drawbridge across the moat, which is kept full of water. In fact, you can't raise or lower it anymore, it's a fixed bridge. But the portcullis is still operational.'

'I can't imagine anyone could enter by surprise,' observed M. Allou. 'Are there any other windows, lower than the ones I can see here?'

'No. Those were put in two centuries later, but nobody dared go below the second floor—and what floors they are!—except for the interior courtyards, of course. As for the exterior walls, up to a height of ten metres there are only arrow slits. And anyone thinking of climbing over the walls would need a very long ladder indeed, since the moats are very deep.'

'Yes, I see.'

'What's more, about fifty years ago, the windows themselves were reinforced with steel shutters. No one, monsieur, absolutely no one, can get in unless the portcullis is raised. Can you see that?'

'Wait a minute. I'm surprised there's no other way in except through the portcullis. After all, when everyone wants to leave—which must have happened from time to time, over the ages—there has to be a way to get in and out when the portcullis is lowered?'

'You're right in theory. There's a postern gate in one of the walls, just above water level, which you can only reach by boat. But it has to be ruled out.'

'Why?'

'It hasn't been used for about ten years. The wood has become swollen, the lock has rusted and now it's totally unusable.'

'Are you sure?'

'Alas, yes. I showed it to the police. It was my last hope... But I was forced to admit it can't be opened. You would have to break it down to get in.'

'But there are still the chimneys...'

'No. They all have iron spikes inside. So, you have to admit, the castle is sealed. Any rational person would have to agree.'

'So it would seem.'

'The terrible thing, monsieur, is that even though I feel my reason is intact, I still can't believe what happened. Apart from secret passages, there's no way to get in.'

M. Allou frowned.

'They only exist in fiction,' he said. 'In real life, they're either no longer secret, or they've collapsed.'

'You're quite right. There was a very old plan of the castle which showed them, in fact. You can read about it here in this cutting. It says that a methodical search was carried out, which found that they'd all been walled up a long time ago. Even after they removed stones from the entrances, they found that the passages themselves had collapsed and nobody could have gone more than a metre inside.

'And that's not surprising. If there had been a passage in working order, Saint-Luce would have told me. That's the Comte (1) de Saint-Luce, the owner. The castle has been in the family ever since it was built.'

'And he was happy to live there?'

'Not at the present time, as you will see. He visited from time to time... What a strange man....'

Pierre Henry had stopped. With his chin on his hands, he stared into the distance, lost in his memories. At last he murmured:

'I know I'm going to have to tell you....'

'Why are you hesitating?'

'Because I'm not sure my reason can take it. I recollect certain things... And yet I'm sure!'

He slammed his fist on the table and a determined expression appeared on his face.

'Yes, I'm sure of my recollections! In that regard, monsieur, I'm not mad! I wouldn't see things so clearly otherwise... I'm not so afraid that I'll take leave of my senses.'

He fell silent again. M. Allou prompted him with a question:

'How did you come to know each other?'

'He wasn't a childhood friend. I met him in India, six years ago. I was hunting tiger, elephant and *gaur*—a bullock more dangerous than a buffalo. It was my passion.

'Saint-Luce was the same. We found ourselves camping in the same village and decided to go hunting together the following day.

'That was the day I saved his life. He was trying to pursue a wounded tiger in the bush, which is always foolhardy. But Saint-Luce never backed down in the face of danger. The creature had doubled back on its tracks to lie in wait for its pursuers, which happens sometimes. She sprang suddenly and trapped him under her paw. My rifle had jammed, so I approached with my pistol drawn.

17

'To cut a long story short, we both got out alive.

'Afterwards, we drifted apart.'

'Why? Something like that should have brought you together.'

'I didn't like him as a person… at least, not entirely. I admired some aspects: his physical courage for one, which was greater than mine.

'But he was too moody and too easily discouraged. You know, in the bush, when you don't know exactly where you are, you don't need someone you can't rely on. He was forever going too far, rashly, then finding himself lost.

'And there were other things which disturbed me. I don't know if it was sincere or due to cynicism, but he despised any form of sentiment. One evening, one of the boys went to fetch water and didn't come back. I was concerned, but Saint-Luce sneered, "Anyone would think there weren't any boys left."

'I didn't like that. I left soon after.

'Yet that strange personage, so full of contrasts, fascinated me and I couldn't put him out of my mind.

'When I returned to Europe two years later, I tried to track him down. He'd given me a Paris address.

'That's how I found that, having returned from Africa less than a month before, he'd retired to his castle in Saint-Luce. When I was told it was close to Paris, I dreamt—having just returned from the bush—of the lush countryside of the Île-de-France. Ah! If I'd only known, I'd have avoided the damned place like the plague!

'Maybe I should have written to him first, asking if I might visit. But, in the sort of life I'd been leading, one quickly forgets the social graces. And, after the great service I'd rendered him, how could I have imagined he'd be anything other than overjoyed to see me?

'I'm telling you all this, monsieur, even though there might not be any direct link to current events. Much of what I've said goes back four years. But that was when the first terrible mystery of the castle occurred, which was one of the few times in my life when I was truly frightened. And I can't put it out of my mind.'

'Keep talking, monsieur. I want to know everything that happened, particularly if the characters are the same as today.'

'They're the same, monsieur.'

'So please continue.'

'I went to find the castle. The first taxi driver I spoke to in Versailles knew the place well, but had never seen any of the inhabitants.

'"In any case, they won't let you in and you'll have wasted a trip. It's a really grim place," he said. "I don't want to discourage you—a fare's a fare, after all—but there are better parts of the countryside to visit, and you'll never get to see the castle."

'"Why not?"

'"I took a foreigner there the other day, who'd read about it in a guide-book and wanted to visit. They shut the door in his face, without any explanation."

'I had to insist he take me there.'

CHAPTER III

A BIZARRE WELCOME

'The taxi stopped in front of the gate in the wall, behind which could be seen the towers of the castle.

'My first impression was a bad one, as you can imagine. The wide, desolate moorland contrasted with the trees (seen through the gate in the wall) under which it was already dark... I'd lived in the bush, but this was different. What was difficult to bear about the dense thickets was to see them surrounded by walls; it gave the impression of a forbidden zone, of an evil spell. Trees shut in, monsieur... I don't like it, it feels wrong.

'On top of that, the light was that of a sad autumn evening.

'Standing back now, I can recall those impressions even more vividly than at the time. They linger in my subconscious and were heightened by subsequent events.

'Because those events are what I'm going to talk about, I'd like you to check with the newspapers about any investigations in which I didn't take part. I have a lot of detailed information at home, but I assume it's under surveillance and I can't go there at the moment.'

'It's easy to get access to the archives of any of the daily papers,' said M. Allou. 'What were the exact dates?'

'The twentieth and twenty-first of October, four years ago.'

'So we'll ask for all the editions between the fifteenth of September and the fifteenth of November.'

'Oh, you don't need all those.'

'Probably not, but one never knows. The events—which I've yet to hear about—could have had origins and consequences you yourself don't even know about. It's better to have everything in hand.'

M. Allou called a busboy over and gave him instructions.

'Please continue,' he said.

Pierre Herry gave a start. He seemed to have gone back to reflecting on the past.

'I was reliving that late afternoon, monsieur, where my fate may well have been sealed. Did I hesitate to ring the doorbell? I don't recall. Maybe I'm imagining premonitions today which I didn't feel at the time.

'I do remember the sound of the bell when I rang it, because I was surprised by its loudness. I should have expected it, however, because the castle was so far away. It was like a church bell.

'"Be patient," the driver told me. "It always takes them several minutes to answer."

'I took advantage of the delay to pay him, and he left. I was assuming I'd be spending the night in the castle. Because of our experiences together in the bush, Saint-Luce and I, I was expecting a warm welcome and possibly an extended stay.

'After a few more moments' wait the gate finally opened and I saw a servant in his fifties.

'I recognised him without ever having seen him, because Saint-Luce had spoken often about him. He'd entered service with my friend's father thirty-five years ago, following a family tradition—for the Laurents, from generation to generation, had always served the Saint-Luces.

'So, my friend had told me, this man had never imagined in his entire life doing anything other than serving a master. His unswerving loyalty had only ever been tested once, with regard to big game hunting. He had insisted on accompanying Robert de Saint-Luce to India.

'But the very first time the unfortunate fellow had heard from afar the low growl of a hunted tiger, he became so pale that the comte— who, as I told you, seldom showed signs of tenderness—had taken pity on him. It had been necessary to face facts: Baptiste Laurent possessed no physical courage, even though he was a good marksman and should have been able to hold his own.

'The unfortunate fellow, apparently, cried with shame and said he'd never have believed he could be so afraid. He became ill and had to be shipped quickly back to France.

'There's a photograph of him in this cutting. You can see he has a round, rather plump face with a ruddy complexion and clear blue eyes: a classic Burgundian.

'You can see him here next to the gendarmes. Stocky, almost fat. A camera effect makes him appear bigger than he actually is.

'What has been captured accurately is his air of astonishment which you mustn't allow to fool you. He's no more stupid than the next man. He was wearing the same expression that evening when he opened the gate, even though he was trying to look severe.

'"What do you want?" he asked gruffly. "We don't welcome visitors here!"

'"Oh, Baptiste, I haven't come to visit."

'The sound of his own name had the same effect as it would on a guard dog: his tone softened.

'"Does monsieur know me?" he asked.

'Now he was wearing a welcoming smile. Profiting from the pleasant disposition, I grabbed my suitcase and entered authoritatively. He immediately looked worried.

'"Monsieur le Comte has given me strict orders not to admit anyone under any pretext whatsoever."

'"He wasn't thinking of me when he said that. I'm an old friend of his and I take full responsibility."

'I thought at the time that I had the right to speak thus, but it was presumptuous of me, as you shall see.

'Baptiste resigned himself to guiding me—that's the right word—through the labyrinth of the park. You can probably guess the impression the castle made on me: one of those beautiful things one admires without wishing to own it. As I went over the bridge I looked down at the green water of the moat... It didn't seem to have changed since the Middle Ages.

'Once inside, I had to climb two seemingly interminable flights of stone stairs to reach the second floor where all the residential rooms were located, they being the only ones with windows. Depressing though the view of the park had been, it was preferable to the views over the interior courtyards.

'I was led into a room which I later learnt was known as the "small salon" as it was a quarter of the size of the others. I sat down apprehensively in what I assumed to be an historic armchair.

'Saint-Luce entered shortly thereafter, providing me with my first surprise. Not that he had changed much physically: his face still resembled that of a bird of prey.

'The photo on this cutting is a good likeness, even to the hard glitter of his beady eyes. You can imagine the body that goes with it: tall and thin, with muscles rippling under his clothes.

'And the very fact that he hadn't changed physically made his attitude that much harder to accept. After you've shared a life of adventure with someone, slept under the same tent, and run the same dangers together, it's normal that you rush to meet when you see each other again.

'Which is what I started to do, but I stopped dead before his obvious reticence. So all we did was simply shake hands.

'"I didn't expect to see you," he said, using the formal "vous" mode of address. "No doubt your letter went astray."

'I'm attempting to imitate the cutting tone he used, monsieur. It was the kind of phrasing you would use just before a duel.

'Surprised, I pointed out we'd used the familiar form of address back in the bush.

'"As you wish," he replied, using the familiar "tu." But the tone he used was one of indifference rather than friendship. I remained silent, which must have made him feel awkward, as he continued in a less hostile tone:

'"It's truly a pleasure to see you again. Have a seat. I'm sure you can give me an hour of your valuable time."

'He must have seen the suitcase at my feet and realised my intentions.

'"I can only stay for twenty minutes," I replied, "for I was foolish enough to send my taxi away and it's getting dark. It's a two hour walk back to Versailles."

'He hesitated before he said: "Please stay for dinner."

'"Thank you, but that would make it worse when I leave."

'"Look here, sit down and we'll sort it all out."

'His tone had by now become even friendlier. Was it possible that I'd mistaken preoccupation for hostility? Or had he begun to realise how much his initial greeting had surprised me?

'"That settles it," he announced. "You'll sleep here. There's no other choice."

'Needless to say, I refused. But he'd already rung for his servant and Baptiste, despite my protests, took my bag away with him.

'"I don't want to force myself on you," I protested.

'"I don't know what you're talking about, old man."

'Now there was a lot of warmth in his voice and he sounded like the friend I'd known before.

'"Yes," he continued, "If I'd wanted you to leave, nothing could have been simpler. We're equipped with the telephone here and I'd simply have called for a taxi. If I didn't ask you straight away, it was in your best interests. I have guests here you won't find at all amusing, my poor fellow."

'He was attempting to make a joke of it, but not succeeding. There was something in the tone of his voice which made me suspect there was another, more serious reason.

'I would have liked to leave. But his demeanour was now so warm it would have been churlish on my part to insist.

'After a moment, I asked: "And just who are these annoying friends?"

'"A Serbian couple named Carlovitch. The wife is quite beautiful if you like the Slav type—which I don't much. Her French is quite passable, but she rarely speaks. And he never does."

'I didn't ask him why he'd invited them, if that were the case.

'"In any case," he added, "you're about to meet them. It's just about dinner time. Let's go into the library."

'I followed him.'

The magistrate placed the package the busboy had just brought in next to him and said:

'Go on.'

CHAPTER IV

THE SACRED STATUE

'Tell me, monsieur, have I struck you as being a reasonable man so far? Please be honest.'

'Well, to be frank, I haven't noticed anything abnormal in what you've said so far. On the contrary, everything appears very clear.'

'So you'll believe me if start to talk about events which are much more extraordinary?'

'Well, at least I won't attribute what you say to loss of reason,' replied M. Allou prudently.

Pierre Herry held his head in his hands once again and meditated for a few minutes. Was he composing what he was about to say or was he about to succumb to his emotions? Eventually he continued:

'Where was I?'

'You were following Saint-Luce into the library.'

'That's right. The room was empty, but I didn't notice that right away because of its huge size and the lighting. Two large candelabras had been lit and the slightest breath of air made the shadows in the remote corners flicker.

'I sat down beside an immense Renaissance chimney and the Carlovitches entered the room shortly thereafter.

'The wife was young and beautiful, even though the photographs don't do her justice because of her darkish complexion. Her eyes, raised at the corners like those of a cat, were totally expressionless. Her cheekbones, slightly too prominent, added to her charm.

'It was her body, feline in every movement, which exerted the greatest seduction.

'I don't remember the man nearly as well. You can probably find a photograph of him in one of the newspapers, although, come to think of it, I don't remember seeing one, even though I looked.

'The first impression was of a giant, and all you noticed was his sheer size. It was only later you realised with some surprise that, unlike most giants, he wasn't at all pleasant.

27

'Thinking back, I think it was because he never looked you straight in the eye and he put you off at the outset with his limp handshake.

'I can only give you physical impressions because, as Saint-Luce had warned me, they almost never spoke. When they did, it was with perfect enunciation except for a slight slurring of the "r."

'Having no idea why they were there, you can well imagine that conversation wasn't easy. Every attempt I made, on topics of general interest, failed.

'Thankfully, Saint-Luce was in a very talkative mood and I was able to pepper him with questions.

'I told you he'd just returned from Africa, where I'd never been. As you know, the native *fauna* there are very different from Asia and so, therefore is the hunt. He told me many interesting facts.

'I noticed, particularly at the dining room table where the lighting was better, that Sonia Carlovitch, although she spoke very little, listened very attentively. She followed everything my friend said with her eyes; if I express myself thus, it's deliberate: the look in her eyes was as nuanced as her gestures and the inflections of her voice.

'As interesting as Saint-Luce had proved to be, I would nonetheless have preferred to talk to the young woman. I was surprised he didn't talk to her more; whether she was one's "type" or not, she was sufficiently beautiful that anybody would have been interested in her. But he seemed to have forgotten she was there; I tried in vain to make amends, but my discreet compliments made no difference and she ignored me completely.

'Such indifference, monsieur, irritated me and attracted me at the same time. I believe I started to fall in love with her at that very first meal; and perhaps, in the end, my constant looks at her were noticed...

'As for the giant, he only stopped eating long enough to roll breadcrumbs in his enormous fingers.

'After the meal we returned to the library.

'I felt like an intruder and promised myself I would leave the next day. I made a vague allusion to that effect, which was met by a rather feeble protest from Saint-Luce.

'When I claimed that I had business to attend to in Paris, he didn't insist:

'"Obviously I'm disappointed," he said, "truly disappointed, because it's been such a long time since we've seen each other. But I understand and I mustn't be selfish. If you have important matters to attend to, I haven't the right to keep you here."

'I lingered a bit longer in the library, however. Not wishing to join in the conversation, I stood up and walked around the room examining the ornaments on display.

'One of them suddenly attracted my attention. It was a small and extraordinarily beautiful stone Buddha, the likes of which I had never seen. I won't bother you with the archaeological details, monsieur. All you need to know is that, for a specialist like myself, there were certain details which were truly unique.

'And, having discovered one more curious than the rest, I turned suddenly to Saint-Luce to enquire whether he'd noticed it.

'I was at the other end of the room from him and his other guests. The light was fully on him and I saw something I hadn't expected.

'Sonia and he exchanged glances, glances both smiling and—how to put it?—tender? No, that's not quite it. "Conspiratorial" is the word I'm looking for.

'Goodness knows, there's nothing strange about a well-built man and a pretty woman looking at each other like that, but after the indifference affected by Saint-Luce during the meal and what he'd said about his guests beforehand, I had a right to be surprised.

'Was he afraid of the husband? My eyes sought out the latter and found him standing by the fireplace, his back towards me, skimming through the pages of a magazine. The light there was too feeble to read by, which caused me to suspect something unnatural about his attitude. He seemed deliberately not to be watching.

'Of course, that was only an impression and it was all over very quickly. Saint-Luce had somehow sensed my look and turned abruptly towards me. He addressed me in a very detached manner:

'"Ah! You're looking at my Buddha. Pretty little piece, isn't it? It's a sacred statue, old man, more sacred than any of the others. If any Hindu were to learn it was here, either he or I wouldn't survive for long! But, luckily, no one knows about it."

'"Where did you find it?"

'"In a small temple, a couple of years ago, after we'd lost touch. I wanted it as soon as I saw it, but there were a lot of old *bonzes* who wanted to prevent me taking it. I made arrangements, not just to let

29

me take it, but also not to talk about it afterwards."

'There was the same sneer on his face as he spoke these words as there had been when the boy had gone missing in India. I felt the same unease and the same desire to leave.

'Maybe he sensed that, or maybe he recalled our separation in the bush, for he came over to me, suddenly very cordial:

'"My poor friend, it seems that whatever I say scandalises you."

'He laughed, but now it was a youthful, radiant laugh, full of charm. I've never seen anyone change character so quickly. As I said before, in the hunt he combined astonishing physical courage with unpredictable mood swings.

'His voice was so cordial and so innocent that I began to have doubts. Maybe the cynicism was just an attitude, born of a juvenile desire to mystify? I started to laugh myself, without thinking about it more deeply.

'He and I started to converse again, but since the other guests remained stubbornly silent, I decided not to bother them anymore and started to head for my room.

'Just before I left, Saint-Luce confided in me:

'"Don't be alarmed if you hear a loud noise later on. It'll be the portcullis coming down."

'Knowing how courageous he was, I was surprised at such a precaution.

'"Just as in the Middle Ages," I replied, smiling.

'But he didn't seem to find my little joke amusing and shook my hand in silence.

'Fortunately, Baptiste showed me to my room, otherwise I'd never have found it. It was on the same floor as all the other rooms, but intersecting corridors created the effect of a labyrinth, misleadingly as it turned out. For, despite first impressions, the floor plan was actually quite simple.

'Shortly thereafter, I heard a violent grinding noise as the portcullis came down.

'I read for a while, then climbed into bed. But I couldn't get to sleep. Not that I'd seen anything extraordinary as of yet, but a number of things had surprised me, if not made me uneasy.

'My friend's welcome, so frosty at first and so warm later on. The incomprehensible presence of the Serbian couple. The looks

30

exchanged between Robert and Sonia.

'And also, it must be said, the lugubrious aspect of the castle itself. In the bush, danger took another form…maybe no more open, but at least more normal.

'A light breeze stirred the foliage of the park. Then it stopped. All was silent. Not the silence of the bush, where something is always stirring, but a total and absolute silence I've only known in the European countryside or on the great moors.

'And it was then, monsieur, that I heard it….'

CHAPTER V

IN THE NIGHT

Pierre Herry had stopped. He stared at M. Allou as his hand reached for the other's arm.

'This is the moment, monsieur, when you have to believe me if you think I've appeared reasonable so far. Remember, I've hunted big game, so I don't suffer from childish hallucinations. I heard....'

'What, then? A cry?'

'Ah! If it were only that... But I must tell you, first of all, that I have extremely acute hearing—almost freakishly acute. Do you see those two people over there at the other end of the room? They're speaking almost in whispers, yet I can hear every word.'

'That's not possible,' exclaimed M. Allou. 'I'm not hard of hearing, yet I can only see their lips move.'

'They're discussing the sale of a restaurant in the Rue du Temple. Go over there and check for yourself.'

M. Allou went over to the window as if to look out at the street and came back.

'You're right! That's astonishing!'

'It's quite possible that I was the only one in the whole castle to hear it, on that night at least. I can't be sure, but I believe so. Because, even for me, the sound was almost indiscernible. And the breeze, up to that point, had been strong enough to hide it.'

'So what was it?'

'How to describe it? Not exactly a howl, more like a sneering laugh, but not human. The cry of a wild beast. If I'd heard it in the bush I wouldn't have been afraid. But there, in the castle, in civilised surroundings...'

'And what animal would you say it was?'

'I don't know. Nothing I ever hunted.'

'And where did it come from?'

'Ah! Therein lay the mystery. Naturally, I assumed at first it was coming from outside, so I opened my window. But I didn't hear it any more clearly, whether it was coming from afar or from within the castle.'

'Did you test the latter hypothesis?'

'Yes. I opened my door and went out into the corridor. There again it made no difference. It was still just as faint.'

'All you had to do was to go farther along the corridor. Because I assume there were no windows to the outside?'

'No.'

'So you could have determined whether the sound disappeared or not, and therefore whether it came from the countryside or the castle.'

'I'd had the same idea, monsieur, and I started to go farther, but very slowly, keeping my hand on the wall for fear of getting lost. I wasn't used to the apparent complexity of the corridors. No doubt if I'd closed my window, the results would have been more conclusive, but I'd forgotten to do so and I'd also left my door open to be sure of finding my own room again. I was expecting to go far enough along the corridor to come to a firm conclusion. Once I know where I am, I travel easily at night. Obviously, I didn't want there to be any light for fear of waking people up.'

'I understand. And what did you deduce about the howls?'

'Actually, I wasn't able to go any farther. At the first intersection another sound, this one completely different, caused me to stop. It was the sound of a door opening, then being closed very carefully. Only someone with my keen hearing would have detected it. And then I heard—or sensed—footsteps, but very light... bare feet on the stone floor. Then another door opening and closing, with the same caution.'

'What did you do?'

'I didn't dare advance any further. Not out of fear, for sure, because there was nothing mysterious about the new sounds—and I've never been afraid of a known danger. Out of discretion, purely and simply. I sensed there were secrets I wasn't supposed to know.

'I returned to my room and, realising I wasn't going to sleep, I lit the candelabra. It was two o'clock in the morning.'

'What about the howls?'

'They'd stopped. I heard them again later, at about four o'clock, for a few minutes. Then the breeze started up again and I wasn't able to hear any more sounds.

'Dawn arrived eventually and I fell asleep for an hour in an armchair. I was awoken by the formidable noise of the portcullis being raised. It was already daytime.'

'And that was all?' asked M. Allou.

There was a note of disappointment in his voice which Pierre Herry detected. In his curiosity the magistrate had no doubt hoped for more.

'As far as that night was concerned, yes. It may not sound like much as I described it, but having lived the moment in that sinister castle, I can assure you I won't forget it. Thank heavens nothing else happened and I'd only heard the beast.'

'Did you ask for any explanations that day?'

'Yes, after much hesitation. It seemed to me that it was my duty to warn my friend. Not that I was predicting danger. But mysteries are always disturbing. And, I must admit, I wasn't the same person inside that damned castle. My hand never shook before, even when I was charged by an elephant. But I lost my nerve in that place. I'm not cut out for that kind of danger. You asked me before whether I was guilty or innocent and I told you I didn't know. Now you understand why!'

Once again M. Allou frowned, seized again by the fear of being duped. So, when he spoke, it was in a noticeably drier tone:

'Continue your story. What was the result of your investigation?'

'Oh, investigation is too big a word. I simply spoke to Saint-Luce. And perhaps it would have been better if I hadn't.'

'Why?'

'Because, as far as the cries were concerned, I wasn't telling him anything he didn't already know.'

'I remember very well our first conversation that morning. I'd eaten alone in the dining room. I scrutinised Baptiste's face, but it only registered its habitual astonishment and placidity. Nothing had occurred to disturb him the previous night.

'Saint-Luce came in, but I said nothing to him then. Rightly or wrongly, I was suspicious of the doors. The Carlovitches were roaming around with their ears pricked up.

'He noticed how pale I was. I told him evasively that I'd hardly slept, due, no doubt to the different bed. A pitiful pretext for an old hunter like myself. No doubt he didn't believe me, for I saw his expression darken.

'"Are you still planning to leave today?" he asked.

'"Yes."

35

'Just as on the previous evening, he didn't insist I stay.

'I asked if we could visit the park. We walked beneath the great trees, whose golden leaves were already rotting underfoot in the dampness. I chose a spot where the thicket was less dense, yet I could still be assured of solitude, to stop and speak to him.

'"I have to tell you, old friend, that I've just spent the worst night of my life," I began. "In the light of day it seems rather ridiculous…and I don't want to frighten you unnecessarily…"

'"Say what you have to say," he replied sharply.

'"Well, I heard some mysterious howls—."

'I barely got the words out of my mouth, for I saw him turn pale. So pale, monsieur, that I can hardly describe it. I've never seen a face so rapidly drained of colour, like the face of a corpse.

'It was even more striking because I had never, even in the direst situations, seen Saint-Luce so much as twitch a muscle.

'He stared at me in silence. Embarrassed, I continued in a lower voice: "The howling of a wild animal, but far, far away."

'I stopped and the colour slowly returned to his face. He looked down and, after a long silence, murmured:

'"So you heard it as well. You're sure it wasn't a hallucination?"

'"Quite sure."

'"Besides, we couldn't have imagined the same thing."

'"So you did hear something? I thought it was so soft only I could have heard it."

'"No, not last night. On other occasions, when it must have been louder."

'"Were you able to identify it?"

'"Oh, I heard too little…almost nothing."

'"And you didn't try to track it down?"

'"How could I…? Although I did try. It's one of the mysteries of the castle. Up until now, I was the only one who knew about it."

'"What about Baptiste?"

'"He would have said something."

'"How long has this been going on?"

'"Up until the time I met you in India, nothing had happened. On my return I stayed seven months here and that's when I first heard it."

'"Often?"

'"No, five or six times, maybe. Then I left for Africa. But when I got back, less than a month ago, it started again... I've heard it four times since. I wondered if it were a hallucination, and tried to convince myself it was. After all, there's no reasonable explanation. If there'd been a wild beast roaming the countryside for the last two years, the shepherds would have noticed, if only by the damage to their flocks. Wouldn't they, Herry?"

"'One would think so."

"'So, I clung to the idea of a hallucination. When you told me just now that you'd heard it as well, you saw my reaction."

"'Yes, but I think it's unworthy of you to let fear get the better of you. You have to search methodically."

"'I've tried."

"'No, not seriously. You only thought about a wild beast. But, as you yourself admit, if such a creature existed it would be common knowledge. I think it's more likely that someone, for one reason or another, is amusing themselves by imitating a howling animal. That's the approach I would take."

"'I've thought about that as well, old man. I've lain in wait in the park at night, trying to track down at least the direction of the noise."

"'And?"

"'All to no avail. Whenever I heard it, it was too faint to identify the direction. I even asked Père Antoine, discreetly, of course."

"'Who's Père Antoine?"

"'You must have noticed, on your way here, a large sheep barn about three hundred metres from the gate."

"'How could I not have noticed? It's the only building on the horizon."

"'That's where Père Antoine raises his sheep. He's often up at night, either guarding his flock during the summer months, or when a new lamb is born."

"'So what?"

"'He's never reported strange noises, although it's true he's a bit hard of hearing. In any case, old man, if it is a human who's amusing himself, why is he doing it? If he were truly trying to frighten me, why not make a louder noise? Last night, you were the only one to hear it. So he would have gone to all that trouble for nothing."

"'True enough."

'As we talked, we were getting closer to the gate. As I looked around at the vast, desolate moor I heard a faint tapping noise which, it seemed, had escaped Saint-Luce's notice.

'I reached the gate and looked through it. I could see a flock of sheep approaching several hundred metres away. After a while they drew level with us and I saw the old shepherd.

'He was of medium height and was wearing the traditional smock. His face was covered in white hairs, so much so one could hardly differentiate moustache, beard or eyebrows. Behind him I noticed a large, rough-haired black dog.

'The man walked slowly, swinging his shoulders. One sensed that under his clothes was one of those twisted, knotty peasant bodies which conserved its terrible strength until death.

'"Is that Père Antoine?" I asked Saint-Luce.

'"Yes," he grunted.

'"Suppose I were to talk to him?"

'"It's utterly useless. I've tried several times to no avail. And with a stranger he'll say nothing."

'"Come with me anyway. I'd like to know where he spent the night."

'And, without waiting for a reply, I opened the gate and went out. It seemed to me that my friend followed me grudgingly.

'Seeing him, Père Antoine stopped, raised his hat and stood there motionless. One sensed in him an ancestral noble, respectful but without the familiarity of old servants. Between Saint-Luce and the shepherd, it was the latter, curiously, who appeared more distant.

'On the other hand, it was I whom the dog was looking at in a hostile manner. As I approached, it opened its jaws as if to bark.

'Ah! Monsieur, you can't imagine the extraordinary impression it made on me. I saw its jaws moving with the normal rhythm, but no sound came out! It seemed, for a moment, as if I'd gone suddenly deaf.

'Startled, I looked at Saint-Luce. "The dog is mute. Curious, isn't it?" he growled.

'We'd stopped, face to face with the shepherd. Amongst all the hairs covering his face, his eyes formed two pools, light but not brilliant; the rather vague look of someone who stares for a long time at the sky and the horizon.

'"Good day, monsieur le Comte," he said in a hoarse voice.

'"Good day, Père Antoine. How are your flock?"

'I noticed that Saint-Luce spoke in a loud voice, as if talking to a deaf person. In fact, as we talked, I noted that the shepherd, while hard of hearing, was far from deaf and we could converse without getting tired.

'"Converse" is not the right word, for we did all the talking. He replied in monosyllables. It was obvious he wasn't much accustomed to speaking.

'After a few observations about the weather I asked:

'"Have you been raising sheep here for a long time, Père Antoine?"

'"For about fifty years, monsieur. I started young."

'"Isn't it tiring, at your age, to spend nights outdoors?"

'"Used to it. When cold, sheep stay in barn. Almost went in last night, though."

'"Why?" I asked, intrigued.

'I hoped he'd been afraid of something. But no. He answered calmly:

'"It were cold. Stay in from now on. Cold season starting."

'"Did you sleep close by?"

'"Over there, monsieur. By the acacia."

'He indicated a miserable tree, three hundred metres from the wall, but on the other side from the castle.

'Upon hearing these words, I let out a nervous laugh and Saint-Luce looked anxiously at me, as if I'd gone mad. No, I—like you, no doubt, monsieur—had simply been thinking about the dog, the mute dog. Surely, when he tried to howl, he must emit a strange and feeble sound? And I was laughing out of sheer relief...

'Or, at least, that's why my laughter rang out in such a bizarre fashion, as I tried to convince myself. But I wasn't being entirely sincere with myself. There are times, as you know, monsieur, when the heart refuses to be convinced by the mind.

'I looked at the black, rough-haired dog standing at the feet of its master.

'"A strange creature," I said. "Does it ever bark?"

'"No, monsieur. Something missing in throat."

'"Surely it howls, sometimes."

'"Never, monsieur. Mute. Totally."

'"How long have you had it?"

39

'"Two years."

'Two years... That coincided with the start of the mystery.

'I looked at my friend. He raised his eyebrows, as if to indicate that, after all, I might be right in my hypothesis. Then he took me by the arm:

'"Let's go," he said. And, in a lower voice: "Maybe it is the dog, after all."

'But I wanted to be sure. I pulled my arm away—Saint-Luce wanted to drag me towards the castle—and spoke to the shepherd again.

'"Is it a faithful companion?"

'"Oh! Yes, monsieur."

'"I ask you that because I'm a little afraid of dogs. This one looks mean and I wouldn't want to meet it alone in the countryside."

'"Not a chance. Never leaves my side."

'"Even at night?"

'"Night same as day."

'My unease returned. No matter how weakly the dog howled, the shepherd standing right next to it would have heard....

'"Night same as day," I repeated mechanically.

'This time, it was Saint-Luce who burst out laughing, saying to Père Antoine:

'"When you're asleep, you can't watch over him!"

'And, without waiting for a response, he moved away, forcing me to follow him.

'Once we were back inside the park, he continued:

'"So it's just the dog roaming at night."

'"Then why didn't you think of that before?" I asked.

'My objection appeared to hit home, for he stayed silent for a moment. Then he confessed:

'"You're right. I don't really believe it. I was trying to convince myself... No, if the dog was in the habit of leaving him, Antoine would have realised it in the course of two years."

'"Can you trust Père Antoine's word?"

'"I believe so. But I don't really know him. I've lived here for such a short time. What I wouldn't give for it to be that dog! I'm obsessed by this mystery, and if I gave you a cold welcome last evening, it's because of that."

"'Because of that? I don't understand."

"'Listen, I'm going to tell you everything. You know I can be courageous?"

"'Absolutely."

"'Yet my nerves are being slowly worn down by this mystery. And now I'm afraid."

"'Why do you stay here?"

"'I can't even explain that to myself. Some unhealthy attraction, no doubt, strange things dragging one towards the abyss. It's a sort of dizziness, as if in a nightmare. You want to run away. But you can't. I just didn't want you to see my fear."

"'I understand, old man."

'We were close to the castle by now. Looking up, I saw Sonia at one of the windows. Saint-Luce followed my gaze and grabbed hold of my arm.

"'You mustn't say anything about this to my guests."

"'Understood."

"'Nor anywhere outside."

"'Rest assured. But I intend to stay in the area and carry out a discreet investigation."

"'In the area? Where would that be?"

"'On the open moor, for heaven's sake. I've done it often enough not to be afraid."

"'And what would be the purpose?"

"'Surveillance, notably of the shepherd…and his dog. By the way, I intend to question Père Antoine again. Maybe he has heard something and is too afraid to say so."

"'Possibly."

"'For now, I shall pretend to leave and come back right away."

"'You're risking your life," said Saint-Luce, in a low voice.

"'What are you talking about? There's a mystery, but there's no danger."

"'You know very well there is. It's not curiosity which is driving you, but unease. Remember, Herry, I've always been able to sense danger."

'That was true. In the bush Saint-Luce possessed an unerring instinct for danger. I did too, by the way, but not to the same degree. It comes from proximity to wild beasts.

41

'"And you have a sense…" I murmured.

'"Yes. Of something stalking me, something which will shortly—it's imminent—pounce on me."

'I didn't argue, for I, too, had the same feeling.

'Saint-Luce stopped and thought for a moment, then put his hand on my shoulder:

'"Don't leave today."

'It wasn't out of politeness, I can assure you. There was something hoarse in his voice which moved me strangely. Yet I protested:

'"I've made up my mind, old man. You have guests who don't seem to appreciate my company."

'"You're imagining things. They never speak more than that."

'"How is that possible? You've certainly chosen cheerful company."

'I said it jokingly, to mask the fact there was a serious question there. For I was indeed asking a question obliquely. The presence of the Serbian couple intrigued me greatly.

'Saint-Luce seemed not to hear. He repeated his request in more urgent tones:

'"Don't leave today… Having spoken of all those things has left me feeling anxious, uneasy. Don't leave me alone, old man."

'If you'd known Saint-Luce in India as I had, monsieur, those words, uttered in that tone of voice, would have moved you as well. I'd often seen him depressed, as I told you, but never afraid.

'I looked at him. He was pale, even white, just as when I had revealed my discovery of the night before. The muscles of his face were drawn and his jaws were clenched. With his eagle-like profile, he looked about to ambush the enemy and defend himself to the death.

'"I'll stay as long as you wish," I replied.

'"At least a few days."

'"If that's what you want. Just tell me when I can leave."

'"Thank you."

'There was a note of real relief in his voice.'

CHAPTER VI

LISTENING AT DOORS

'We resumed our walk. He'd asked me to change the subject, so we talked about our hunting days. We passed a half-demolished cabin surrounded by railings which reminded me of the time we captured a young tiger which Saint-Luce had brought back to Europe.

'"I had to have it put down," he told me. "Once it reached adulthood it attacked me."

'"Did you keep him close to you?"

'"He followed me everywhere in the park, like a dog."

'That shows you what kind of man Saint-Luce was, monsieur. On the day I'd rescued him, he'd been under the beast's paw with its mouth a few centimetres away. Yet he'd had no apprehension about the creature he'd brought back. He knew no physical fear, which made his moral weakness so disconcerting.

'We were approaching the castle again, and I asked him to show me around.

'Only the southern part was inhabited and completely separate from the rest. Like all the castles of that period, this one was composed of distinct parts, only communicating via narrow, iron-bound doors.

'The ground floor consisted of vast vaulted rooms which served as cellars or storage areas. I visited half a dozen of them, all alike.

'"There's no point in visiting the others," said Saint-Luce. "They're all very similar, except that in some, stones might fall on your head and in others you might be devoured by rats and spiders."

'As you can see from the photograph, monsieur, the first floor walls are only pierced by arrow slits, yet that was where the servants were housed.'

'What servants?' asked M. Allou.

'Baptiste, whom you already know about, and the cook.'

'The cook?'

'Oh! I don't think she's of any importance to the story. I've only seen her two or three times. She's fat and has white hair. There's something shifty about her, for she never looks you in the eye. I know one mustn't jump to conclusions. It might be shyness rather than hypocrisy.'

'Had she been working there a long time?'

'Thirty years, probably.'

'She could have married Baptiste,' said M. Allou with a smile.

'The same thought occurred to me and I mentioned to Saint-Luce. He told me the absence of such a formality hadn't seemed to bother them much. She was ten years older than he and the youthful spark which leads to such arrangements had long gone. Each was more concerned with saving money.

'And at their age, even though they occupied adjacent rooms on the first floor, they probably ceased any night visits a long time ago. And Saint-Luce gave me another reason preventing their marriage. Baptiste, because of the length of time his family had been in service, was fiercely loyal. Clémence, even though she'd been there a long time, had no such tradition.'

'Was it that obvious?'

'It was very clear. She might have had some affection for Saint-Luce's father, who was a real homebody, but he was in no doubt that she didn't care for him and his mixture of madness and malice. His lifestyle shocked her, but he kept her on anyway because he didn't like change and she was a good cook. And, in any case, it wouldn't be easy to break in someone new. It was also partly for those reasons that Baptiste hadn't married her.

'Still chatting, we continued our tour.

'The master's rooms were all on the second floor. Saint-Luce showed me several of them, notably his own. He walked past a room with its door closed, saying:

'"That's the Carlovitches' room. I don't want to disturb them."

'My curiosity got the better of me, despite myself. I tried to recall the events of the night before. Do you remember, monsieur? After those mysterious howls I detected a strange movement in the corridors: two doors being very quietly opened and closed, one after the other, and stealthy footsteps.

'I tried to recall the exact spot where I'd stopped in the corridor. It wasn't difficult: I'd turned right onto the main corridor where my host's room was situated, and also that of the Carlovitches. I carefully

44

noted the distance between the two rooms, and it seemed to me that it corresponded to the duration of the footsteps. It was very likely they had gone from one room to the other.

'Besides, what other possibility could there be? Those were the only two occupied rooms and it was hardly likely someone would have gone to an empty room. What would they have done there?

'It had also occurred to me that someone had gone to the library, which was also nearby, to pick up some object left behind. But why, in that case, all the furtive precautions? The individual who had roamed in the night hadn't wanted to run the slightest risk of being heard, I was sure of that.

'From the Carlovitches' room to Saint-Luce's. The idea—I didn't yet understand why—gnawed at me strangely. One can be in love a long time before admitting it to oneself.'

*****

'There's not much more to tell about that day, monsieur. There was only one discovery, but it may be an important one.

'Lunch was just like the previous night's dinner had been: Saint-Luce and I spoke amongst ourselves and Sonia listened "with all ears," but in her case it was more like "all eyes."

'How can a look be simultaneously mysterious and expressive? It seems contradictory…. But no, Sonia's look merely showed interest. But was that interest driven by curiosity or passion? Approval or blame? Nobody knew. I've often seen wild animals follow my gestures; sometimes they've run away; sometimes they've stayed to fight even harder; sometimes they've left their tranquil spot.

'As for the giant, he seemed both deaf and blind. His enormous face was devoid of expression; his whole body represented a solid mass—a tree trunk. And yet I watched him, hoping to catch a sign of jealousy, or at least annoyance. But nothing….

'I tried to talk to him. He affected—or so it seemed to me—not to understand a word I was saying. He indicated by a growl what I should repeat.

'Needless to say, I quickly tired of that and stopped talking to him.

'I had the curious impression it was me he was jealous of, not Saint-Luce. Yet the furtive look I'd observed the night before seemed to

45

represent a greater risk to Sonia's fidelity than my own advances, however indiscreet. But Saint-Luce was better than I at hiding his feelings and appeared to be completely indifferent to Mme. Carlovitch.

'After coffee I returned to my room and remained there until four o'clock.

'I don't know whether you've noticed, monsieur, how naturally silent my movements are.'

'I hadn't made a particular note of it,' replied M. Allou, 'but, now you mention it, it is effectively the case.'

'It's characteristic of the hunter, born of many nights lying in wait. On the stone floors of the castle all footsteps resonate and a door shutting can set off an echo. And the corridors are so quiet at night you can even hear the sound of bare feet.

'But in my case, monsieur, you wouldn't hear me, even wearing slippers. It's not deliberate, I swear. It just comes naturally from an instinctive fear of noise. So it was that I exited silently from my room.

'I wanted to go to the library to consult a couple of technical books I'd previously noticed. I was obliged to pass by Saint-Luce's room, right next door, and as I did so I could hear two people talking. I recognised the voices of my friend and Sonia.

'At this point my conduct became inexcusable, monsieur, I readily admit. My only excuse is that the mystery was weighing heavily on me and starting to become an obsession. I sensed danger, particularly for my friend.

'Was it, as I told myself, the desire to protect him? Or was it curiosity—or even something worse? I myself didn't know. There are instances, monsieur, when one doesn't know oneself. Does that seem normal to you, even with a reasonable man?'

'Quite normal,' said M. Allou.

The magistrate was becoming less sceptical about his companion's fear of madness. He seemed sincere. Far from manifesting disorder in his thoughts he was, to the contrary, recounting a perfectly coherent story and going to great lengths to be as precise in the telling as possible. It was as if he were trying to affirm his sanity.

'I'm sure you've guessed what I did, monsieur. From the corridor I could merely hear the sound of voices. Even that was thanks to my prodigious hearing, for the doors of the castle are massive. Yes, I stepped forward and pressed my ear to the door.

'It was Sonia who was talking and I could hear her very well, even down to the rolling r's in her speech. She was more passionate than usual.

'"You have to agree, Robert," she said. "It's not for his sake—I don't care about him. It's for mine, selfish though that may be. I want to be rich, do you understand? I'm tired of living in misery, wearing torn dresses and dining on charcuterie bought from the corner store—."

'"But, Sonia—."

'"Let me finish. You say you love me, so think of me in those squalid surroundings with kitchen odours wafting up the stairs and the noise of families squabbling and their children screaming."

'"Sonia, stay here with me."

'"You know that's not possible. He would kill me. Robert, why can't you help him? He's competent enough as a chemist. You'd be quite satisfied. Why do you refuse?"

'Saint-Luce's voice hardened, just as in his worst moments. I could imagine the ferocious look in his eye.

'"Because I've no desire to keep your marriage going! I want to separate you from him, do you understand? If I hate him, it's not just because he's your husband; I find him vile, boorish and abject. Sonia, you can't stay with such a man. I've spent years waiting for you, years trying to forget you by risking my life in many countries. I want you for myself and I won't let anyone get in the way. Particularly someone like him. He's cheated and stolen…"

'Sonia didn't deny it, but lowered her voice to the point that even I could scarcely hear it and simply repeated:

'"He'll kill me…I can't do it."

'There was silence. And, fearing they might suddenly come out of the room, I retired stealthily to the library.

*****

'Shall I tell you about the dinner? I'm not sure about what I observed. It's possible that my imagination blew a misleading impression out of proportion.

'It seemed to me that the first glass of wine I was served had a strange taste. Only slightly so, and I forgot about it almost immediately.'

'Was it poison?' asked M. Allou.

'Oh, certainly not. More like a sleeping draught. I say that because I was rapidly overcome by a feeling of tiredness I tried in vain to fight off. You might argue that, after a sleepless night, that wasn't surprising. But I've spent many nights lying in ambush without sleep. I only needed a few hours dozing during the day to recover, just as I had done that afternoon.

'No, nothing could explain the fatigue that I tried to resist.

'During the course of the evening, I went to examine the sacred Buddha again. Was it just archaeological curiosity which attracted me? Certainly it was a strange work. But, in my heart of hearts, wasn't I hoping to discover another secret?

'This time I didn't find anything abnormal about it and I soon returned to the others. All three of them seemed very gloomy. They were seated facing the fire, each seemingly lost in their own dream.

'When I spoke, Sonia and Robert sat up startled; they seemed to have forgotten me. Only Carlovitch continued to sit there placidly.

'"I'm going to retire," I announced. "I don't know why, but I can't keep my eyes open."

'"I shall be doing the same, soon enough," replied Saint-Luce. "I'm asleep on my feet."

'I didn't think at all about sleeping draughts, and had already forgotten the impression I'd had at dinner.

'Once in my room I went straight to bed. My eyes were starting to close even as I undressed. I would dearly have wished to stay up and lie in wait for those strange and terrible cries from the night before, but I felt utterly unable to do so.

'Nevertheless, just before I fell asleep, I heard the loud creaking noise of the portcullis coming down. Why did it seem more sinister than the night before? Are there really such things as premonitions or was I, in my half-sleep, just the victim of the unease I'd felt throughout the day?

'I considered getting up and locking my door. But I was ashamed of my cowardice and resisted the temptation.'

CHAPTER VII

THE ATTACK

'In any case, even if there's no such thing as premonition, I certainly believe in instinct. I've seen animals sense danger, and savages, too. And, through living in the bush, I have as well.

'One evening, while I was sitting in a forest in India, I suddenly started to shiver. I grabbed my rifle even before I could think, and there it was: a tiger crouching a few feet away, just about to pounce.

'That night in the castle, monsieur, the same thing happened. I awoke with a start, certain that someone was lying in wait for me in the shadows and that my life was in danger. Without even registering what form the danger took, I leapt out of bed, bounded forward and crashed into someone standing there in the room.

'Needless to say, I tried to pin his arms to his sides, which was fortunate for he was holding a heavy club in his right hand. I wanted to grab him by the wrists, but he was stronger than I. And yet look, monsieur....'

Pierre Herry took a coin from the table and effortlessly bent it in two with his bare hands.

'Yet he was stronger than I! The fight in the darkness was fierce and silent. All I heard was the man's breath. Several times he managed to get his right arm free and strike me with his weapon. But I parried with my left and tried to attack his face, without success.

'Suddenly I received a blow on the temple which sent me reeling and I fell to the floor. Although dazed, I still had the *sang-froid* to roll away from him, which gave me the advantage as he didn't know where I was, and there was nothing to stop me attacking him from behind.

'I tried to work out where he was by his sounds, but my strongest suit—my sense of hearing—had been affected by the blow. All I could hear was a ringing in my ears.

'How long did I lie there in wait? Seconds? Minutes? Impossible to tell. Eventually, I forced myself to get up. The ringing had stopped,

49

but I couldn't hear anything.

'Had the fellow left the room, or was he standing there motionless, waiting for me to move? My anxiety didn't last long, at least in that regard, for I was soon alerted to another, more specific danger.

'Calls for help were coming from the corridor. It was the voice of Saint-Luce and I confess it made me really afraid: for him to be calling for help, the danger must be great indeed. I knew his courage and his pride.

'Nevertheless, I rushed to help him. The corridor was dark, but by now I knew the layout. His door was wide open and in the doorway I ran into a man standing there. I grabbed his arms as before, but from his exclamation I recognised Saint-Luce and identified myself.

'"A light!" he said.

'Luckily, I had matches in the pocket of my dressing-gown. When I struck one I could see nothing abnormal save for a red mark on my friend's forehead. I went into the room and lit the candelabra.

'At that moment Sonia came running, dressed in a kimono.

'"Those c-cries," she stammered. "I heard… What's happened?"

'She was as white as a sheet.

'Saint-Luce had sat down and was trying to get his breath back. I examined him more carefully.

'The wound to his head was superficial. I could see red marks on his wrists, signs of the intense struggle he'd fought.

'Eventually he spoke. From his few words, I inferred he'd suffered an aggression similar to my own.

'He'd been attacked in his sleep, or, more precisely, he'd been awakened by the sound of the door opening. Once up, he'd encountered his assailant, enormously strong and armed with a heavy object.

'"That," Saint-Luce added, pointing to a heavy club from the Middle Ages, which I'd seen in one of the display cases and which was now lying on the floor.

'He'd fought and, like me, had received a blow which he'd been able to parry somewhat. It was at that point, sensing he'd been vanquished, that he'd cried for help.

'But suddenly, by virtue of a desperate manoeuvre, he'd regained the advantage, disarmed his assailant and thrown the weapon away.

'And so the attacker had fled. And Saint-Luce, still numb from the blow, hadn't thought to pursue him. It was a moment later, when he'd started out for the corridor, that I'd run into him.

'He explained it all in four or five sentences.

'"Let's find him!" I cried. "He can't have left the castle. Grab your revolver."

'I was about to leave, candelabra in hand, when another complication arose.

'Sonia started to scream:

'"Don't leave me! Don't leave me!"

'But she refused to accompany us.

'"Stay with your husband," I said. "Why isn't he here, for that matter? Didn't he hear Saint-Luce's cries for help, as you did?"

'She didn't reply. Clutching with both hands at the mantelpiece behind her, she seemed about to fall.

'Taking no notice of her action, I continued:

'"Let's go and warn him."

'She followed me as far as their room, where I knocked on the door. When there was no response I opened it. The room was empty!

'"Where is he?" I asked.

'"I don't know," she murmured.

'I noticed there wasn't one large bed but two small twin ones.

'"Didn't he go to bed?" I added.

'"I don't know," she responded again. "I was asleep."

'"Then let's find him," I retorted. "He can't have left the castle. The portcullis hasn't been raised, has it?"

'The question was addressed to both her and Saint-Luce, but I already knew the answer. I would have heard it.

'They shook their heads in unison.

'"Let's go and wake Baptiste," added Sonia. "He knows better than anyone. The winch is in his room."

'We went down to the first floor and knocked on Baptiste's door. He didn't respond right away. The calls for help from the floor above hadn't reached him and he was still asleep.

'Then I heard him get up and come to the door to ask what we wanted. As soon as he heard Saint-Luce's voice he drew back two bolts and opened the door to us.

'Seeing the three of us standing there, his habitual look of astonishment gave way to one of fright. He stood there, his mouth

51

open, not uttering a word.

'His master quickly summarised the situation and asked if he'd raised the portcullis.

'"Oh! No, monsieur."

'And he indicated the winch and the chain, which was fully played out.

'I looked at the bolts on the door, which were enormous. Impossible to draw them back from the outside. Nobody had entered his room while he was asleep and, in any case, the noise of the portcullis would have woken him up.

'"So," said Saint-Luce, "Carlovitch is still in the castle. Let's look for him."

'We lit more candelabras and, all together—Baptiste behind us—we started to search, thoroughly and methodically. I even insisted on visiting the cook's room.

'We had to accept the evidence: Carlovitch had gone! The doors communicating with the uninhabited parts of the castle were bolted from the inside.

'That's when I began to suspect that was where Carlovitch was hiding! His wife had bolted the door after him... But, in order to verify the hypothesis, we would have to accuse Sonia directly.

'So, in order to confront her with the evidence and cut short any protest, I declared:

'"Let's check the portcullis to see if it's still lowered."

'I approached it while I was talking—for we were already on the ground floor. I began to think it was futile, because in the half-light I could see the bars which sealed the entrance.

'But when I got closer, candelabra in hand, I let out a cry: the portcullis had not been lowered all the way down!

'Hearing my shout, the others came over. They could see as well as I that there was enough space at the bottom for a man to have crawled out.

'"Well, that's extraordinary," said Saint-Luce. "The bars are always lowered to the ground."

'"To the ground," repeated Baptiste. "Besides, the chain was fully extended."

'We bent down to look more closely and the mystery was solved. Someone had placed a block of stone on the ground, which had blocked the portcullis from completing its descent.

'"The escape was planned," I murmured.

'"Yes, everything was prepared in advance."

'"But has he left the park?" I asked. "The walls are quite high."

'"The gate in the park wall," replied Saint-Luce, "has only bolts and no lock. It's easy to draw them back."

'"Let's take a look."

'Saint-Luce and I were about to slide under the portcullis when he looked up at Sonia. From the light of the candelabra she was holding, I could see she was deathly white and her eyes were dilated.

'"Don't leave her here alone," I said.

'Without a second thought, I dismissed Baptiste as useless: I noticed how the hand carrying the candelabra was trembling. Before Saint-Luce could protest, I slid under the bars and reached the park. It was pitch black and I naturally hadn't brought a light: for protection I was counting on the stealth of my tread and my acute hearing.

'I quickly arrived at the park gate. When you're a hunter like me, you don't get lost at night if you've visited the park by day. I can get lost inside a house, but never in the open air....

'I felt around for the bolts and determined that they were no longer shut. Returning to the castle, I asked Baptiste if he'd made sure the gate was bolted. He assured me it had been; he always did it at sunset and yesterday evening was no exception.

'It seemed pointless to continue the search. Carlovitch had escaped onto the great moor and there was no hope of finding him.'

CHAPTER VIII

THE BEAST AGAIN

'We went back upstairs and I noticed the telephone on the first floor landing. It had been placed there so as not to spoil the pristine collection of period furniture on the second floor.

'I'd forgotten about it and, as soon as I saw it, suggested:

'"We should call the police."

'"No," replied Saint-Luce.

'He let Sonia climb a few steps ahead and then whispered:

'"It's her husband you're talking about."

'I knew enough to understand and so let it rest. My friend's generosity surprised me, for Carlovitch's arrest would have been an excellent way of getting rid of him.

'But Saint-Luce probably felt he'd furnished enough pretexts for the attack for him not to file a complaint. It was an affair best settled between men, and calling the police would be a form of cowardice. Saint-Luce had his scruples in such matters.

'To be frank, the attack on me was far less justifiable. I may have looked at Sonia rather insistently and tried to engage her amicably in conversation...and perhaps I'd been less discreet than I'd intended. But that was hardly a reason for attempted murder.

'Carlovitch had made his jealousy obvious, even though it was ridiculous. What kind of thoughts went through the mind of this taciturn, dumb Slav who must have noticed that Sonia was distancing herself from him? Hadn't this boorish fellow (to use the description coined by Saint-Luce) been nurturing a secret rancour for a long time?

'If Carlovitch had acted out of an aggrieved jealousy, then even lesser transgressions would have appeared serious to him. And his mad rage had caused him to attack all those he felt had offended him.

'No doubt he must have surprised his wife returning from Saint-Luce's room—just as I had probably done the night before—and grabbed hold of the nearest weapon, the club in the display case in the corridor. His anger had got the better of him.

'He should theoretically have attacked Saint-Luce first, for he was truly the guilty party. But maybe he'd only caught his wife as she returned to their room, without knowing where she'd been. He'd vaguely suspected both of us, Saint-Luce and me; probably me first, because I wasn't his friend and my attitude seemed more questionable.

'When I fell to the floor, he'd thought me dead. And when Saint-Luce disarmed him, his cowardice had returned and he'd fled the scene.

'As my conscience wasn't clear, it wasn't up to me to insist the police be called. And, in any case, I don't like asking for protection.'

*****

'Without answering, I followed Sonia and Saint-Luce into the library, where we sat down in silence.

'Baptiste stoked the fire. The search of the castle, clad only in pyjamas, had chilled us all.

'Saint-Luce ordered him back to his room and the three of us gathered around the hearth.

'We stared at the flames, saying nothing. Perhaps I should have left the two of them together, but the thought didn't occur to me.

'Suddenly I shuddered: I'd just heard the beast howling, just as on the previous night!

'Maybe slightly louder. Only slightly, and I still had to strain hard to hear. I had the normal reflex, useless but instinctive: I leant forward, as if that could help.

'Saint-Luce saw the movement and the expression in my eyes, and immediately realised what had happened. He gave me a look, imploring me to say nothing, indicating Sonia.

'It would indeed have been cruel to add that to her turmoil. Her lips were already bloodless and the added revelation might have killed her.

'I said nothing and the watch continued. Shortly thereafter the clock struck four, and I tried to calculate how much time had elapsed since I'd been awoken. The attack must have taken place at around half past two.

'We waited in silence for the dawn. Ah! Monsieur, what a horrible night! I've known others, in that very castle, and worse, as you shall

56

hear. But that night left a special impression.

'The beast was still howling, monsieur. Oh, not continuously. I would have preferred that and perhaps become used to it. No, the howls came suddenly, ten or so times an hour perhaps, and lasted for a minute or so. Each time, I experienced the same nervous shiver and eventually began to tire.

'I was also afraid Sonia might hear it, but it seemed not, luckily.

'Eventually dawn came up and, with that, the wind rose and I could no longer hear the howling.

*****

'A moment later, Baptiste brought in some warm drinks. I was glad of them and even more glad of the interruption, for the silence had become unbearable and seemed as if it would never end.

'The arrival of the beverages and the resultant movements started us talking. Trivial matters at first, but then Saint-Luce declared:

'"He won't be back."

'"Do you think not?" I asked.

'"He's a coward. The only thing he's capable of is an ambush. And tonight the castle will be firmly shut."

'"Do you plan on staying?" I asked. "Why not go back to Paris?"

'"Because Sonia would be much more exposed there than here. I can protect her better here than in a crowd. We won't leave for several more days. Carlovitch's anger will have subsided and been replaced by fear. He will think the police have been alerted and will try to get a long way from here."

'It was a convincing argument. But if Saint-Luce stayed, then so would I.

'I confess, monsieur, I would have preferred to leave. But there was no point in hesitating, so I declared:

'"You can count on me. I'll leave when you do."

'"Good," replied Saint-Luce, simply.

'I could tell from the tone of his voice that he considered it to be natural, and not the sort of thing you offer thanks for, between men like us.

'But fate decided otherwise. Before leaving Paris I'd left instructions as to where I could be found, and during the day I received a telephone call. My sister had been run over by a motor car and was not sure to survive.

'My sister is all I have, monsieur. Our parents died young and she was, and is, my only affection.

'Duty to friends takes second place and so I left immediately.

'Even so, my initial concern remained. As I was giving Baptiste a little something, I tried to question him.

'"You've never noticed anything out of the ordinary before tonight?"

'"No, monsieur."

'So he'd never heard the howls. I continued:

'"You have a strange neighbour…the shepherd."

'"Père Antoine? He doesn't speak much, but he's not a bad fellow. I've known him since I was a child."

"Is he honest?"

'"Oh, I think so. If he wasn't so close to his money, he wouldn't have any faults."

'"Is he tight-fisted?"

'"Of course. He's a peasant. But that's his only love. Or, at least," he said smilingly, "until the last few days."

'"Now he has another?"

'"Yes, but just platonic. For Mme. Carlovitch."

'"How do you know that?"

'"When she walks in the countryside, you should see how he looks at her!"

'None of that was of much interest and so, because I was in a hurry to leave, I left the matter there.'

CHAPTER IX

A CRIME

'My sister had indeed been badly injured. I passed the night at her bedside and didn't leave her for the next two days.

'On the third day she appeared to be getting better and I opened a newspaper. It was dated October 20th. Take a look, monsieur, and you'll understand my emotion.'

M. Allou searched in the pile of old newspapers he'd put next to him, pulled one out and unfolded it.

There was a headline spread over a quarter page:

Strange disappearance of engineer Carlovitch.
Anonymous letter claims it was a crime.
Police are searching Saint-Luce castle.

'And before that?' asked M. Allou.

'I hadn't seen anything about it.'

The magistrate scoured the earlier papers: there was no mention of the case. Pierre Herry asked him to read the article. M. Allou spread the paper out on the table and started to read in a low voice:

*****

'Versailles, October 19

'Yesterday evening a strange letter arrived in the Public Prosecutor's office. It was unsigned and the author appeared keen to remain anonymous. He seemed to have written the letter with his left hand, which would make identification impossible.

'Why such a desire not to be recognized? Does he fear repercussions? Is it a bad joke? It's difficult to say at this time.

'In any case the accusation made is a grave one. It is no less than an accusation of murder!

59

'Here is a reproduction of the document:

'"Engineer Carlovitch had been living in Saint-Luce castle for a week. During the night of October 16-17, he mysteriously disappeared. The body cannot have been taken outside; search the castle and you will find it, no doubt carefully hidden."

'We called this a reproduction of the document, but that is not strictly correct. We reprinted it with correct spelling, that of the mysterious correspondent leaving much to be desired. But isn't that the custom for anonymous letters?

'All who know the vigilance of the Public Prosecutor's office will not be surprised to hear they reacted immediately to the letter. Less than one hour later, the regional Flying Squad had been notified and a search authorised for that same morning.

'It had already begun when we received the news. Our magistrates are as discreet as they are efficient. Our duty, however, is curiosity, is it not? So, to cut a long story short, our car was in front of the park gate before ten o'clock the same morning.

'An initial disappointment awaited us. A gendarme was on guard and refused us access.

'But we were not going to allow that small detail to deprive us of our story. We had driven past a sort of farm on the way and we now returned to it, hoping to gather information.

'There, we experienced a further disappointment. We found an eccentric personage, an old shepherd with a hairy face and initially quite taciturn. But we know how to be patient when necessary.

'By interpreting his monosyllables, and even more so his silences, we were able to learn some facts about the owner of the castle. He is the Comte de Saint-Luce, some forty years old and seldom seen in the area. He spends his life hunting big game in Asia and Africa. He only returned to the castle two months ago, after an absence of several years.

'Less than a week ago he received two mysterious guests, Engineer Carlovitch and his wife. The latter, Sonia Carlovitch, is still in the castle; it is her husband who has mysteriously disappeared.

'A few days earlier, an unknown man—it was the first time the shepherd had seen him—arrived and spent two nights there. He left by *taxi about ten hours after the disappearance of Carlovitch.*

'There were few other details. But Fate never abandons reporters. We suddenly notice that the gendarme, apparently lulled by our attitude and more interested in following the search, has turned his back on us and is looking towards the interior of the park. At the same time, one of us has made an interesting discovery: behind the sheep barn is a long ladder used in storing forage.

'He signals to us and we quickly take our leave of the old shepherd. It is child's play for us to place the ladder against the wall, out of sight of the gendarme, who still has his back turned. We climb over, despite the three metre height of the enclosure.

'At first, we are somewhat embarrassed by our success. We find ourselves in a veritable virgin forest. How to reach the castle?

'We succeed, not without considerable difficulty. It's not locked. There is an inspector there, but clearly his orders are only to prevent people leaving. They do not cover people entering: for that they rely on the gendarme at the gate. We walk straight in without him saying a word.

'Under the immense stone vaults, the echoing sounds of voices act as our guide. Soon we find a large group and intermingle discreetly with the inspectors from the Flying Squad. The magistrates from the Public Prosecutor's office are too pre-occupied with their meticulous work to notice.'

At this point, M. Allou could not help but smile. He knew perfectly well that magistrates often turn a blind eye, but a journalist must have the good taste not to notice! He continued, still in a low voice:

'We are able to recognise our eminent Public Prosecutor and our remarkable examining magistrate, M. Cordani, accompanied by Commissaire (1) Libot. Next to them is a tall, thin man with the face of a bird of prey. This vigorous-looking individual is the Comte de Saint-Luce himself. Someone else attracts our attention: M. Dupont, an architect who often advises the department.

'Lights are useless, for the search of a historical castle, riddled with hiding-places, is no simple matter.

(1) equivalent to superintendent

61

'The architect is holding a plan which looks old and respectable. We learn that it was supplied by the owner himself, in order to facilitate the search.

'The architect, however, is taking nothing for granted and, measure in hand, is going over every surface carefully to make sure nothing is overlooked.

'There are plenty of possibilities for hiding places inside the thick walls and under the flagstones. Helped by the inspectors, M. Dupont is examining the castle stone by stone checking if any joints are showing less signs of dilapidation, which would indicate more recent displacement.

'They are proceeding at a speed which ensures no detail will escape them. But, to us non-participants, time seems to pass very slowly! Added to which there is an extremely disagreeable odour emanating from the courtyards and rooms where rats have lived and died for centuries, stones occasionally fall from the vaulted ceilings, and the place seems infested by a particularly menacing species of spider.

'After about an hour, we weary of the search and go up to the floors above, which seem like the only ones inhabited.

'The first floor appears empty. The second is much better furnished, to judge by the corridors. We knock on a few doors and, emboldened by the silence, take a look inside. Our curiosity will be rewarded.

'We suddenly find ourselves in a vast library where a very beautiful woman, apparently of Slav origin, is seated by the hearth. We naturally ask for forgiveness for our indiscretion, but merely as a pretext to prolong our stay and ask more questions.

'Unfortunately, she is not very talkative. Nevertheless we learn a few essentials: she does not believe a crime has taken place in the castle; she is fully aware her husband has gone; and she firmly believes it was he who sent the anonymous letter.

'But why, we ask? Why flee the castle? Why take such a revenge?

'But Mme. Carlovitch, tired or feigning to be, refuses to answer any more questions. We learn later that she was only slightly more forthcoming with the examining magistrate.

'She told him she and her husband had quarrelled after he had accused her of being M. le Comte's mistress. He had ordered her to leave, but she never obeyed orders. And, as he left, he had told her he would take his revenge.'

*****

M. Allou paused again in his reading.

'Is it true that Sonia made a deposition, or did the reporters make that up?'

'It's perfectly true, monsieur,' replied Pierre Herry. 'It was confirmed to me afterwards. I'll explain to you later.'

'It seems irreconcilable with that you've told me so far. Either Sonia lied to you that famous night by her actions, or she lied to the investigators. In your opinion, did she or did she not know, while you were looking for her husband, whether he had already left?'

'I honestly cannot say, monsieur. She seemed to be sincere, but you'd have to be mad to take such a woman at face value!'

'Let us continue,' said M. Allou.

And he started reading again:

*****

'As we continue to ask questions, she reaches out for the bell on the table nearby and shakes it. A servant soon appears. His name is Baptiste and she orders him to escort us out.

'Once in the corridor, we turn aggressively on Baptiste. Bombarded with questions, the Burgundian just stares at us with the permanently surprised expression on his face, which is no doubt congenital.

'To force him to reply, we ask him brutally if his master M. le Comte had committed a crime.

'We think he's about to strangle one of us. His eyes are burning with fury and he is stuttering badly, claiming it is an unpardonable calumny. He claims that, on the contrary, his master was at pains to take great care of the Carlovitches. We ask what they were doing in the castle and he claims he has no idea.

'We ask if there was someone else there the night the engineer disappeared and he claims not to take note of the visitors M. le Comte receives. It's pointless to continue.

'Fortunately, he feels it is his duty to mount guard over Sonia Carlovitch, fearing we will return to question her again. Thus we are able to descend the stairs by ourselves, unencumbered by a third party

63

for our next encounter, which takes place on the first floor.

'We have been making so much noise coming down the stairs that a plump face appears at a half-open door as we go by. In a flash, we turn our attention to the newcomer, Clémence the cook, easy prey for reporters. The mere sound of our questions causes the old woman to perspire heavily and she fearfully avoids our gaze.

'She soon abandons all resistance. When we ask if a crime has been committed she says we must not ask such a question without proof. When we ask if her master is capable of such and act, she points out he has spent his life killing—by which she means wild animals—and one thing leads to another.

'When we point out she kills lobsters by boiling them she replies that they make no noise. When we ask if she has rabbits killed, she says they are for eating, whereas her master doesn't eat any of the animals he kills.

'Then she babbles on about the animals M. le Comte has brought back and let loose in the park, transforming it into a menagerie, and even raised a tiger there! He'd almost been eaten, and where would that have left the servants? How would they have got out? They would have died of hunger, but he had never given any thought to that, being an egoist.

'We leave her, not having learnt much except there is at least one person in the castle who believes M. le Comte to be capable of anything. There is no need for us to go downstairs to meet the investigators, they are working their way up, step by step.

'The clock strikes midday and we overhear the Public Prosecutor calling Versailles to send lunch over. From the number of meals he orders, we realise joyfully he has not forgotten us.

'We eat hastily. Will we be finished by nightfall? Yes, because happily the ground floors are much larger than the upper floors in castles of this period and the other parts of the castle are not a high as the one we are in. The afternoon searches are just as tedious as in the morning. The moats are drained, of course, without result. Every chimney is examined.

'Night falls, everything has been inspected and nothing has been found. Which means we can confidently assert there was never anything there.

'Have we been the victim of a practical joke? Too early to say, for the body could have been buried in the park. We will search it tomorrow, with the dogs. A few men will remain on guard overnight.

'The magistrates are waiting for the taxis they have ordered for nightfall. They have become more talkative and we question them. Are they sure there is no body hidden in the castle? Absolutely certain. The architect nods his head in approval. One of the magistrates adds that it might be in the park.

'We point out that even if no body is found, that does not mean that no crime has been committed: the body could have been taken away. They say they will also search the countryside nearby. When we say the body might be farther away, they express doubt, given the lack of a motor car or even a carriage on the premises and the fact that Carlovitch was a giant who could not have been carried far. Furthermore, it would be dangerous to bury him in the countryside because of the risk that the shepherds would notice any freshly-dug ground. The park, with its infrequently visited undergrowth, offers the most effective hiding places.

'That seems obvious, but one of us observes that a motor car could have come from Versailles to take the body away. That argument is rapidly disposed of: Père Antoine, who is a light sleeper and lives by the roadside, had heard nothing. Farther down the road there are other farms, all of which had been visited, with the same result.

'In addition, all the organisations renting out motor cars have been questioned: none had the castle as a destination. All the household provisions are brought in by bicycle.

'We point out that a vehicle was seen leaving the castle the day after the disappearance, a motor car. We are told it was the same individual who spent two nights in the castle, an old friend of M. le Comte named Pierre Herry, whom they intend to question. He had indeed left by taxi, as reported by several of the peasants. The driver had been questioned in Versailles by an inspector and was above reproach.

'At that point the magistrates all leave and we follow suit. Tomorrow morning we shall be here at dawn and will keep our readers informed about what is discovered in the park.'

CHAPTER X

THE LARGE BLACK DOG

M. Allou refolded the newspaper.

'You can see,' said Pierre Herry, 'that I had nothing to do with the disappearance of the corpse... even if there was one, which I doubt.'

M. Allou had already picked up the following day's edition. This time the headline was much smaller:

No corpse at Saint-Luce Castle.
Either a joke or act of vengeance.

He didn't bother to read it.

'So,' he asked, 'they didn't find anything?'

'Nothing, neither in the park nor in the surrounding countryside, despite having brought in quite a crowd. The dogs only found tracks of deer and other small game. It was exasperating. They started out each time barking, and each time it was a disappointment. They used them in pairs, keeping them on the leash, and after a few kilometres, they stopped.'

'So you were there?'

'Of course. But I must finish my story. I promise you I'll be brief.'

*****

'I was at my sister's bedside, as I told you, when I read the astonishing accusations and the report on the previous day's searches. Scarcely had I finished when my servant arrived.

'"Monsieur," he said, "two men were here asking for you."

'"So?"

'"So I told them monsieur had gone, without leaving an address."

'"But why? You knew full well I was here."

He lowered his voice:

'"They looked like policemen, monsieur."

'I became very angry:

'"That wasn't a reason! Why would I wish to avoid the police?"

'"I read the morning newspaper, monsieur."

'"Imbecile! You've compromised me for no good reason. The whole story is a joke!"

'Now I was afraid I'd be implicated in the affair. So I hailed the first taxi I could find and asked to be taken to Versailles.

'I was quite surprised, at first, that Saint-Luce hadn't telephoned me to alert me to the situation. But when I thought about it, it seemed understandable. He must have feared, with reason, that the line was tapped.

'What was I going to say to the magistrates? According to the papers—I'd bought others on the way—neither Saint-Luce nor his servants had said anything about the events of the night, the two attacks against us. Such silence appeared natural on Saint-Luce's part: not having spoken about it at the beginning, a later declaration would have appeared suspect. And nothing strange about Sonia's or Baptiste's silence either. They were under orders from Saint-Luce.

'But the cook? Strictly speaking, she'd known nothing of the attacks and we'd deemed it pointless to tell her. But she'd known all about our searches during the night, because we'd come to her room.

'It seemed to me very unlikely that she hadn't said something to the examining magistrate, which he in turn hadn't chosen to disclose to the press.

'So how did Clémence's deposition compare with Saint-Luce's? What explanations had he offered under questioning? I was very uneasy and hoped I'd be able to communicate with my friend before being interrogated myself.

'It was not to be. As soon as I arrived within one kilometre of the castle, I was stopped by a gendarme. The precaution was pointless, because half of Versailles was trying to invade the park! By being allowed to disperse on the great moor, the crowd could contribute enthusiastically to the searches. Rest assured, if there had been a tomb, they would have found it.

'When I gave him my name, the *gendarme* let me through. But at the park gate I was stopped by another, who led me directly to the examining magistrate.

'M. Cordani was a charming fellow with a blond moustache and soft blue eyes. At the sight of him, my confidence grew.

'He thanked me for coming so quickly to see him and started by asking a few discreet questions. He understood straight away that my visit to Saint-Luce had been a friendly one, which he himself had made no attempt to hide.

'"I need to ask you, monsieur, if you saw anything on that famous night?"

'That was the question I was dreading. So....'

Pierre Herry stopped, somewhat embarrassed. M. Allou smiled indulgently and waved him on.

'Because it involves one of your colleagues.'

'I understood that. But each of us has his own personality... and his own methods. If you made a fool of him, that's none of my business.'

'So I decided to reverse the roles and—in a roundabout way, obviously—become the interrogator. It's a good idea, sometimes, for the hunter to allow himself to be pursued by the hunted, in order to flush them out. Oh! I'm sorry....'

'Keep going.'

'So I replied: "Nothing, monsieur," but with a smile which plainly said "something happened." That way, he could choose which path to follow. It was that of the smile.

'"What do you mean, nothing?" he asked indulgently, as if the word didn't express my real meaning. "Would you contradict your friend?"

'"I meant nothing regarding the crime."

'"Well, at least we can agree on that. You weren't present at the murder, if there was one. But you did nevertheless see something strange, did you not?"

'He seemed so sure of himself that I felt sure Clémence must have talked, which after all was likely. I proceeded to reveal to him, as spontaneously as I could, that we had searched all over for Carlovitch, but had had to admit finally that he had got away.

'"And that surprised you?" asked M. Cordani shrewdly.

'"Oh, no!" I exclaimed. "It's what I expected. I just wanted to verify the fact for myself."

'"Ah!" exclaimed the magistrate. "So his wife's explanations hadn't entirely convinced you? Admit it!"

'That's how I realised that the press had accurately reported Sonia's testimony.

"'Saying I wasn't convinced would be going too far. Let's just say I didn't know her well enough to accept her testimony lock, stock and barrel."

"'You're saying that to be polite," protested the magistrate. "But the fact is you'd noticed the improbability of her story."

'I opened my eyes wide in naïve astonishment.

"'No, monsieur, nothing of the sort. It's just that subtlety isn't my strong point."

'M. Cordani smiled in satisfaction and, taking me by the arm as if confiding in me, said:

"'Just between the two of us, if Carlovitch had indeed left his wife out of jealousy, do you really think he would have left without saying anything to Saint-Luce? That he would have left without seeing him?"

'Now I knew everything that Saint-Luce had admitted and what he had kept to himself. The magistrate had replied very thoroughly to my indirect questioning. He knew nothing of the attacks. I proceeded to speak authoritatively to him, affirming that Carlovitch, for all his size, was nothing but a coward; that he had preferred the petty vengeance of an anonymous letter to an open fight.

'M. Cordani, by speaking so frankly, had shown he trusted me and I was quickly able to influence him. Nevertheless, even though he'd become convinced of the futility of the search, his professional conscience obliged him to pursue every avenue thoroughly to the end.

'He willingly granted me permission to join Saint-Luce. I found him in the library with Sonia. He welcomed me amiably enough, but guardedly, which puzzled me at first. Then it occurred to me: did he suspect me of having written the anonymous letter?

'At face value, the idea was stupid. Everything pointed to Carlovitch who, with the limited choices available to him had tried to cause trouble for his rival.

'But, after all, Saint-Luce didn't actually know me very well. We had only become close recently. He'd noticed the way I'd looked at Sonia and Carlovitch's attack on me proved that he, too, had noticed and was jealous of me as well.

'From Saint-Luce's point of view, wouldn't I have been capable of writing the letter in order to get rid of him as a rival? Once accused of killing the husband, it would be difficult to keep the wife close to him without arousing further suspicions.

'Yes, he may very well have considered that as a possibility; hence the coolness of the reception. I wanted to disabuse him straight away, so I took him to one side to say I hadn't spoken about the howls at night.

'I had guessed correctly. My reticence towards the powers of justice made me an ally, and his face softened.

'"You did the right thing," he said. "Now, more than ever, I want to drop the matter."

'"Why?" I asked, in spite of myself.

'"First of all, there's no point in talking about it, because it has nothing to do with Carlovitch's disappearance."

'"True enough."

'"And secondly, I've decided to sell the castle. It'll be hard enough with all that the papers have written about it. The last thing I need is for it to be haunted as well!"

'"You want to sell the castle? Your ancestral home?"

'"I've had enough, old man. The mysterious howling, the attacks, the police visit... As I told you the other day, all of that has worn on my nerves. I'm at the end of my tether."

'It was plain to see. There was a mixture of overexcitement and despondency which was a very bad state to be in.

'"I'm not built to deal with this kind of fear. I have to have enemies I can fight face to face."

'I understood the sentiment only too well, having experienced it myself in these surroundings. There are dangers against which simple courage is to no avail.

'"You're right," I replied. "In your shoes, I'd do the same thing."

'I glanced at Sonia, seated some distance away.

'"Sonia's staying with me," he said. "They can think what they like."

'And, with a sweep of his hand, he indicated the park, still crawling with police. I admired his audacity.

'"I'll leave you alone," I said.

'I realised from his attitude that he preferred to be alone with Sonia. He made no attempt to detain me, merely asking politely:

'"When shall we see each other again?"

'"Not for quite a while. I'm returning to India in a week's time."

71

"'Good luck, old boy. For me, all that's a thing of the past. I'm staying in France from now on."

"'Goodbye. You're right: leave the castle and sell it.'"

'If only he'd followed my advice....'

*****

'I left the park. My taxi was waiting for me at the gate.

'I had the impression—alas, mistaken—that I would never see the place again and wanted to take one last look at it. I took a few steps in the countryside. The sun was hiding behind the clouds and everything looked sinister.

'Little by little I approached the sheep barn, where I wanted also to bid farewell to Père Antoine. He received me with neither suspicion nor amiability, but with that air of indifference all shepherds show.

"'It's terrible what's happened to monsieur le Comte," I said. "The suspicions of him are really scandalous."

"'Monsieur le Comte should have expected something of the sort," he replied.

"'What makes you say that, Père Antoine?"

"'The day before yesterday he looked very upset. He walked around on the moor all afternoon. I could see him from my doorway as I smoked my pipe, far away, pacing to and fro and sometimes stopping, like a worried man. He only came back at nightfall."

"'Wasn't Mme. Carlovitch with him?"

"'No, monsieur. Since her husband left, she hasn't set foot outside."

'I thought I detected a note of sadness in his voice and I remembered what Baptiste had said.

"'My poor Père Antoine," I replied. "You'll probably never see her again. They're going to leave the castle...."

"'Ah!"

'He nodded his head slowly and murmured:

"'I knew it. I knew she wouldn't be here for long."

'It seemed to me that his look was more melancholy than usual.

"'Does that make you sad, Père Antoine?"

"'Oh, monsieur, that would be ridiculous."

"'Anyway, they're leaving."

"'Together?" he growled suddenly.

"'Why, yes. It seems as though that worries you, Père Antoine."

"'It's all the same to me. It was for her sake."

"'For her?"

"'Monsieur le Comte is not always easy to deal with."

'The shepherd, as I said before, has a rough voice which is easily mistaken for anger. Was there something in his voice... a hatred for Saint-Luce which I thought I'd detected before? I put it to him directly:

"'You don't like him?" That was too direct a question for a countryman to answer. He remained silent.

'Embarrassed, I looked away. My gaze fell on the large black dog. To change the subject, I murmured:

"'What a strange creature."

"'Strange indeed. And, by the way, I misled you the other day. He does howl sometimes."

"'Really?"

"'Yes, in silence."

'There was something naïve about the expression "howl in silence," which might cause some to laugh. Yet I didn't feel like it. The creature had made an impression on me....

"'Are you trying to say, Père Antoine, that it tries to howl? Why have you concealed that from me?"

"'Because I didn't know, monsieur. I noticed it for the first time the other night: the night when M. Carlovitch left. I happened to go into the barn—I don't remember what the time was—and there it was, in front of the door, standing there with its mouth open. I'm used to its silence, monsieur, but that had quite an effect on me."

"'Is its howling as silent as its barking?"

"'Absolutely. I couldn't hear a sound."

'So the sounds I'd heard hadn't come from the dog. And they couldn't have reached me in the castle, with its windows shut tight, without being heard by the shepherd, who wasn't completely deaf.

"'So what did you do, Père Antoine?"

"'I opened the door to check outside. But it was pitch dark, and I couldn't see anything."

"'And the dog?"

"'It didn't even try to go out. On the contrary, it seemed afraid. I shut the door quickly."

"'Did it do it again?"

"'Not the next night. I went down several times to check. It was sleeping peacefully. But then, the night after that, it was worse."

"'Please explain."

"'It was trying to howl, as it had two nights before. But this time it was throwing itself against the door, trying to get out. Needless to say, I didn't open. I just got hold of my gun…and listened."

"'And did you hear anything?"

'The shepherd waited almost a minute before answering. Eventually, he murmured:

"'Yes."

"'What did you hear?"

"'It's difficult to describe. My ears aren't what they used to be, you know. It was like a beast howling…but not quite."

"'It sounded a little like sneering, would you say?"

"'Yes, monsieur. So you've heard it yourself?"

'Without answering, I continued:

"'Was this the first time for you?"

"'Yes, monsieur. And the last. Since then, there's been nothing and the dog is no longer agitated."

'I placed my hand on his shoulder.

"'It's best not to talk about this, Père Antoine. Such things are as mysterious as ghosts. It brings bad luck to tell about them."

'I was trying to frighten him, but it wasn't necessary. At the mention of the word "ghosts" he crossed himself and protested:

"'Of course I won't talk. I only told you because you're a friend of monsieur le Comte, and it's best if he's aware of such things."

"'Yes, and I'll make sure he knows. But for everyone else, silence. Is that understood?"

"'Of course, monsieur."

'From the tone of his voice, I was sure he would keep his word.

"'Then goodbye, Père Antoine."

'As I left him, I started to think the astonishing thing that had just happened. The normally taciturn and tight-lipped shepherd had confided in me. I couldn't understand why.'

'Perhaps,' insinuated M. Allou, 'he'd wanted to tell you something beyond the strict meaning of his words.'

74

'I don't understand.'

'Well, for example, he managed to inform you indirectly that he hadn't left the barn on the night of the attack against you.'

'That's right!'

'Or then again,' continued M. Allou, 'maybe he was hoping you'd repeat what he said to Sonia so that, frightened by the mysterious menaces, she wouldn't follow Saint-Luce.'

'That's possible, too.'

'And, there again, he might have wanted to insinuate that there was something shady going on, corresponding to the anonymous letter.'

'But, in that case, it would be he who—.'

'I don't know,' concluded M. Allou. 'I merely presented you with three hypotheses, that's all. And it's also possible that he was perfectly sincere and simply wanted to unburden himself of a secret which was weighing on him in his solitude.'

M. Allou refrained from mentioning a fourth possibility which he had nevertheless considered: a lie by Pierre Herry himself, who had invented the shepherd's tale in order to demonstrate that even after his departure there was still a mystery surrounding the castle.

CHAPTER XI

WHEN THE BEAST HOWLS FOR THE THIRD TIME...

Pierre Herry had stopped, with a far-off look in his eye.

'I think I've told you everything about the first story,' he said eventually. 'It happened over four years ago and may have nothing to do with the other, far more terrible one. But I hope it was worthwhile to tell it?'

'Apparently so, but we'll see,' replied M. Allou.

'I wanted to demonstrate, above all, that I was capable of recollection and reason. Did you believe me, monsieur?'

M. Allou made a non-committal gesture.

'Answer me, I beg you.'

'I listened...objectively. I didn't try to determine whether you were sincere or not.'

'That's not what I meant. I was simply asking if my way of expressing myself was that of a man whom one might believe. Do you understand what I'm saying?'

'In that case, what I can say is that there is nothing in your way of talking or thinking which would throw suspicion on your reason.'

'That's what I wanted to know.'

(Which means nothing, thought M. Allou. Even lunatics can describe certain moments in their lives with perfect lucidity. On the other hand astute fakers know how to talk nonsense at the right time, without exaggerating.)

'Yes,' continued Pierre Herry, 'it seemed to me that my memories were correct. I've seen extraordinary, incomprehensible things. And since then, monsieur, I've seen things which are impossible. Do you hear me...? Impossible. Things which my reason cannot admit, but which I'm certain I witnessed. Certain! Now can you understand my agony?'

'Continue with your story,' said M. Allou. 'Try to give it the same accuracy.'

'Oh, that will be easy. It's all engraved in my mind. It's all just as clear to me as what I've recounted so far....'

He was becoming agitated as he spoke. To calm him down, M. Allou asked him a precise question:

'How long did you stay in India?'

'Four years, monsieur. There's nothing much to tell except for one incident, which I found striking.

'I'd travelled through many territories in search of big game. One day, I received a message from the local administrator, who advised me to avoid one specific area, where the lives of Europeans were in danger.

'I'd received similar messages during my travels in the bush, which had only ever served to stimulate my curiosity and entice me into places where I wouldn't have gone otherwise. I reacted the same way again. Even so, the message having been rather laconic, I decided to find out more about the danger I might run. I made a detour to visit the administrator who had written to me.

'He explained that, a few years earlier, a sacred statue had been looted from one of the temples in a particularly barbaric fashion. The priests had all been shot with a carbine. One of them, although severely wounded, had survived long enough to describe the attack.

'Such facts usually remain with the locals and don't percolate up to the authorities. Following the theft, several groups of Europeans were massacred as revenge for the original villain.

'In the case of this particular statue, the authorities were better informed. The administrator described it and, as I'm sure you've guessed, I recognised the miraculous Buddha of Saint-Luce castle.

'So the horrible account my friend had given was not a joke. He had really killed to get it, just as he had hinted.

'As I told you, monsieur, that kind of danger doesn't normally frighten me off, but everything to do with the castle of Saint-Luce has left me with a mysterious fear which I dare not ignore. This time I paid heed to the local administrator and avoided the area. .

*****

'That's all there is to tell about my stay in India, monsieur. I'd had no news about Saint-Luce, so when I returned to France a week ago, I had no idea what had become of him.'

78

*****

'A week ago...

'One of my friends, a journalist, had had an unfortunate idea. He thought to please me by publishing an article, on the day of my disembarkation, about my exploits. I had brought back a number of rare animals for the local zoological gardens, as returning hunters often do. There was really nothing there to brag about and my friend could have saved some ink. It's true that the poor devil couldn't have foreseen....

'Never mind. The point is, that's how Saint-Luce knew I was back.

'I hadn't counted on seeing him. What had happened in India had negated any such desire and I didn't think he would be looking to renew our relationship, either.

'And so I was very surprised the next day when he paid me a visit.

'My first impression was that he had aged. Not that he was wrinkled or that he stooped. It was something else: an air of weariness seemed to have spread over his whole body. His voice, too, was less sharp and less clear.

'We exchanged the usual formalities which occur after long periods of separation.

'"Where are you living now?" I asked.

'"In the castle."

'I was surprised to learn that he'd kept it, contrary to the decision he'd announced previously. He noticed my reaction and murmured:

'"After such a long time in the family...."

'"Of course. Do you live there alone?"

'"With Sonia."

'"Ah! So she stayed... Doesn't she find it hard?"

'"No, she likes solitude. Sometimes we come to Paris."

'"And Carlovitch?"

'"No news. He's disappeared from circulation."

'There was a question on my lips. To delay asking it for as long as possible—for I knew very well he wouldn't want to broach the subject—I enquired about Baptiste, Clémence and Père Antoine. Nothing new to report there.

79

'Eventually I could hold back no longer. Lowering my voice in spite of myself, I enquired:

'"And the howls?"

'"They continue."

'"Frequently?"

'"My hearing isn't as good as yours, so I only hear them twenty or thirty times a year. You would surely hear them more often. Although now…."

'He didn't finish his sentence.

'He'd sounded worried enough. But, behind his words, I detected an even greater concern.

'"What else is there?" I demanded brusquely.

'"Ah! You guessed… It might be nothing: just a joke, or a form of revenge like the anonymous letter. But everyone in the castle is getting nervous. You were right, I should have left… Anyway, you can be the judge."

'From his pocket he pulled out a page from a notebook, folded in four, and handed it to me. I read it:

'"Return the statue or you will die. Place it on the moor next to the Square Stone. When you have done that, tie a handkerchief to the bars of the gate."

'I'm reciting from memory, monsieur, but the tone was like that and the words were very similar.

'"The Square Stone," explained Saint-Luce, "is located at about a kilometre from the castle."

'Without replying, I examined the letter. It had been written using the left hand, like the anonymous letter which had unleashed the massive search years before. Was the author again afraid of being identified? Was he therefore known to Saint-Luce?

'Still, there was one difference which struck me. You read in the newspaper report just now that the first letter, four years earlier, contained spelling mistakes. The one I was holding in my hand was free of such errors.

'I thought, naturally, of Carlovitch. He could have perfected his knowledge of our language over the last four years.

'"Carlovitch?" I suggested.

'"Possibly…. If I could be sure, I wouldn't be worried."

'"Obviously, acting alone…."

"'But did he know the origins of the statue?" objected Saint-Luce.

"'Of course. You told me about it in the library, in the evening of my arrival. He was sitting—I recall it vividly—in a dark corner, skimming through a magazine which he obviously couldn't read. I have to assume he heard the story too."

"'If that's the case, then why did he wait four years to exact revenge?"

"'Maybe he's been absent during that time."

"'Possibly...."

"'You don't seem convinced," I observed, in surprise.

"'You still don't know everything. This business is much more complicated than that. The day this letter arrived—."

"'Arrived how?"

"'Oh, the most normal way possible. By post, with a Versailles stamp. As I was saying, the day it arrived I was in my room with Sonia. My reaction was to shrug my shoulders. We had lunch and went for a walk. I gave orders to Baptiste about a re-organisation of the ground floor. To cut a long story short, I received the letter at ten o'clock in the morning and didn't return to the library until five o'clock in the afternoon. I automatically glanced in the direction of the statuette...."

'Saint-Luce paused and lowered his voice:

"'It had disappeared!"

"'And you haven't recovered it?"

"'No."

'I thought for a moment and then exclaimed:

"'There's no mystery! Sonia found the letter during the day, read it, and—less courageous than you are—followed instructions and placed the Buddha by the Square Stone."

"'I did consider that. The letter had been on a table in my room and Sonia admitted reading it. But she swore she hadn't touched the statuette."

"'Maybe she didn't dare...."

"'Knowing how much grief the theft had caused me, she wouldn't have hesitated to confess. And I couldn't have blamed her for her good intentions."

"'Maybe it was Baptiste. He's very devoted to you."

"'No, I questioned him as well."

81

'"Damn! It is getting complicated. Then suppose it was your anonymous correspondent who helped himself? As you say, you were out all afternoon."

'"Then how do you explain this second letter, received a week later?"

'Saint-Luce pulled another letter out of his pocket, similar to the first, and handed it to me. It read:

'"Our patience is running out. Place the statue as ordered and do not forget our threat."

'I kept the letter in my hand, not knowing what to say.

'"I have my own theory," said Saint-Luce. "It is in fact vengeance, but in a more terrible form than you can imagine. Do you remember how I obtained the Buddha?"

'"Yes. And someone told me about it when I was in India."

'There was a catch in my friend's voice when he replied.

'"Ah... Do they suspect...?"

'"The authorities only know it was a European. But the natives know more."

'"How could they?"

'"There was a survivor."

'At these words, I could see perspiration break out on his forehead, his pupils dilate and his face go as pale as on the day I first told him about the howls.

'As I told you, this man of great physical courage was a moral coward and this was further proof.

'In a hoarse voice he repeated:

'"A survivor?"

'"Yes. Severely wounded and probably dead since, but a survivor, nonetheless. And he talked."

'"I was well-known there," murmured Saint-Luce.

'"Do you think that's where the threat is coming from?"

'"I had a suspicion before. Now I'm sure."

'"But that doesn't explain the disappearance of the statue."

'"Yes it does. Let me explain. Haven't you been struck by one thing: the threats weren't all that terrible...they offered me a chance to save myself."

'"Precisely. That indulgence seems in contradiction to the hatred you presume."

'"Quite the opposite. It's a very refined form of cruelty. They have given me an order which I cannot possibly carry out! Do you understand? Instead of killing me right away, which would be nothing, they want to inflict this mental torture where I can see death coming and, needing but a simple gesture to avoid it, feel paralysed. Just as in my nightmares!"

'There was desperation in his voice and I was deeply moved.

'"I defy you to find another explanation," exclaimed Saint-Luce.

'"What you should have done was deposit a letter at the Square Stone explaining why you couldn't carry out the order."

'"I have never in my life asked for mercy," he retorted.

'But he soon admitted, avoiding my gaze, that Sonia had done so.

'"And what happened?"

'"The letter remained there, unopened. They guessed the contents. What else could it have said?"

'"I suppose so. I need more time to think."

'"There are days when I do nothing else."

'"Days? So the letters aren't recent?"

'"The first arrived a month ago, the other a week after that."

'"And since then?"

'"There have been two more, the last one the day before yesterday."

'"Show them to me."

'The first one read:

'"*You are wrong to ignore our threats. Next week we will begin to act.*"

'"That's rather vague." I said.

'"Read the last one."

'This time I went pale myself as I read it. It said simply:

'"*When the beast howls for the third time, you will die.*"'

83

CHAPTER XII

DREAD

"'The beast," I murmured.

"'The beast," he said in a low voice, "has already howled once."

"'When?"

"'Last night."

"'And was it like what I heard before?"

"'Ah, no, old boy, no. The same kind of howl—or so I believe, because I could hardly hear it then. The same, but ten, twenty times louder. Something horrible! And something I'm very familiar with."

"'That you're familiar with?"

"'Yes, I heard it in Africa. It's the sneering howl of the hyena. I had that impression before, but the howls were so faint and I couldn't be sure... It seemed so unlikely."

"'And where are they coming from?"

"'The park."

"'The park or outside?"

"'Just outside, perhaps."

"'What are you talking about? You're going to drive me mad as well. There aren't any hyenas around here, or I would know about it."

"'It's not a hyena," he replied in a subdued voice.

'For a moment I was stunned.

"'Saint-Luce," I protested, "am I going mad, or are you? Didn't you just tell me a moment ago...?"

"'Yes, that it was the howl of a hyena. But with something I never heard in the desert. It's the same howl, but—how best to put it?— emphasised. That's it: emphasised. More tragic and more horrible... A savage sneer... The hyena's hasn't got such bitterness. It's not so menacing."

"'Are you sure your nerves aren't deforming your senses?"

"'Now you're the one going mad, Herry," he retorted. "Do you really suppose there's a hyena roaming around in the area?"

"'You're right. I'm losing my mind. So it's a man?"

85

"'Logically, that's what we should assume. Or it's a beast I don't know.'"

'I had the impression, monsieur, of living in a nightmare. I had, from time to time in the past, seen him perturbed. But never in the state of terror he was exhibiting before my very eyes.

'He leant towards me:

"'I don't want to die, Herry! Not at this time, when I'm so fortunate. I'm happy when I'm with her. It's probably wrong of me to say that. I seem to remember...."

"'It was nothing. A crush, long forgotten.'"

"'I couldn't live without her. I'd kill her before I'd let her go!'"

"'So, has she thought about leaving you?'"

"'She's frightened, do you understand...? Last night, when the howls rang out, she was doubled up in her armchair, frozen in fear. She could die from her emotions.'"

"'Let her leave!'"

"'Never,' he cried in a hoarse voice. 'Besides, who says she wants to?'"

"'You did, just now.'"

"'All she said was that we should leave the castle.'"

"'And she's right.'"

'Saint-Luce got up and started to pace nervously around the room.

"'You're as stupid as she is, my poor friend,' he said. 'You're assuming the castle is haunted and once we're in Paris there'll be nothing to fear. But, if there's to be any hope of defending myself, it's there behind the walls, the portcullis and the arrow slits. Someone was able to get in one day and steal the statuette. Now, it isn't possible. The portcullis is permanently closed, do you understand? It's raised only if someone wants to leave. In Paris, or anywhere else, I would quickly be found and it would be all over. You can be sure someone followed me here.'"

'He became more and more carried away and his speech became incoherent. I made him sit down.

"'You're right,' I said. 'You're safer in the castle.'"

"'If I stay,' he replied in a hoarse voice, 'she has to stay as well.'"

"'You're right,' I declared, to calm him down. 'Besides, if she wanted to leave, it would be with you. If you stay....'"

"'She's dying of fear there. When I left earlier today, she almost" screamed with fright. I have to return before nightfall."

"'She'll calm down when you get back."

'He didn't reply. I pressed him:

"'Don't you think so?"

'He replied, very quietly:

"'I don't believe she will."

"'Obviously, if something horrible happens again...."

"'Even if nothing happens."

"'Why?"

'He got up, came over to me, and said, very distinctly:

"'Because she's lost faith in me. Doesn't trust me any more."

"'Lost faith?"

"'She's afraid, even when I'm there."

"'Afraid for you!"

"'And for herself as well. And why should she believe in me," he continued bitterly, "when I no longer believe in myself? I'm a nervous wreck! I'm at the end of my tether."

'I didn't quite understand what Sonia wanted. To go away alone? She mustn't even think about it. At that moment, Robert growled:

"'She's not going to leave!"

'When it concerned her, his willpower was still there. One sensed he would be capable of anything.

"'So?" I asked dully.

"'So I've come to ask for help. That's the second time it's happened. Do you remember before, when you saved me from under the tiger's paw, I hadn't cried for help? At that time—now so far away—it seemed I never would. You believe that, don't you?"

"'Yes, Saint-Luce, I'm sure."

"'Since then, those damned howls have made me another man. I called out once, four years ago, during that attack. I thought at the time that I had changed. Do you remember my attitude afterwards, sad and sombre, even though Carlovitch's departure should have made me mad with joy? It was shame that I felt. Now, today, I'm asking for help again."

"'You know very well that I won't refuse you."

'He spoke with a brief flash of pride:

"'It's not just for me, but for her as well."

"'But will she accept my presence?"

87

'He bit his lip. The answer cost him dearly:

'"It was she who asked."

'I tried to conceal the profound joy I felt when I heard those words. Sonia had faith in me. That, at a stroke, revived and increased the sentiments I had before.

'"I'll come," I replied simply.

'Saint-Luce, now calmer, returned to his chair and declared:

'"There are only two men I esteem enough to ask that of them. You, and Gustave Aranc."

'"Aranc?"

'"Have I never spoken of him?"

'"I don't believe so."

'"It's true I haven't seen you for four years. He was young then and living in England. He's my nephew, my sister's son."

'"And why do you hold him in such esteem?"

'"Because he's a big game hunter like you and me. Not for very long—he's young, as I said—but he's already proved himself. He's just spent two years in Africa. Between the three of us, we can brave any danger."

'His voice sounded firmer as he invoked our solidarity. He was with his own kind again, and gathering strength from that.

'"Are you thinking of asking him?"

'"It's already done. I talked to him this morning."

'"Does he live in Paris?"

'"Versailles."

'"And you explained your reasons?"

'"Oh, he knows everything already. He returned to Europe three months ago. He's been a frequent visitor to the castle."

'"And has he heard any howls?"

'"Last night? No, he wasn't there."

'"But before that?"

'"He never mentioned it. Was it to avoid frightening me?"

'"And has Sonia ever heard them?"

'"Not before last night."

'"And Baptiste?"

'"No more than Sonia."

'"And Père Antoine?"

'"He told me he'd heard them once, several years ago. Around the time Carlovitch disappeared."

"'It's all very surprising," I observed. "It seems as though, since I left, you're the only one to have heard them."

"'I'm afraid so," murmured Saint-Luce.

'When he said that phrase, it wasn't meant to signify the customary "I believe so." He really did seem to be afraid.

"'It's either one thing or the other," he continued. "Either the danger's only intended for me, or I'm a victim of hallucinations."

"'Yes, and I'd prefer the latter; you too, I presume?"

"'I? Not at all!"

"'Yet previously you did. Do you remember your fear when I told you I'd heard the howls myself?"

"'That was then. It wasn't the same thing. I felt solid then, morally. Today I fear madness more than death."

"'Maybe the others did hear something and didn't dare to tell you. Why didn't you ask them?"

"'Don't you understand? I didn't want them to think me mad!"

"'All right. Last night, however, did everyone hear it?"

"'Ah! Everyone: Sonia, Baptiste, Clémence and even Père Antoine."

"'And what does your nephew know, exactly?"

"'Everything else: the history of the statue, the threatening letters, last night's event."

'I looked at my watch. It was four o'clock.

"'Better be going," I said, "so Sonia doesn't get scared."

"'So, you're thinking of her," he said, in a strange tone.

'I looked at him, but then he added in a neutral voice:

"'Call a taxi. I don't want to mix with travellers."

"'And bring your revolver," he added, as we were leaving.

'It would have been careless indeed to have left it behind.

'We reached the castle at around five o'clock.'

CHAPTER XIII

SOMEONE GOT IN!

'I recognised the wild moorland. Then, from afar, the high walls dominated by trees. And, higher still, the towers.

'What Saint-Luce had told me, disturbing though it was, had not affected me as much as that sight did. At that precise moment, the past ceased to be a memory and joined the present in such away it seemed as if I had never left, and the tragic adventure had continued without interruption, getting worse from each day to the next.

'At the sound of the rising portcullis—a sound which had, contrary to my expectations, remained vivid in my ear—and the creaking which reverberated under the vaulted ceilings, it was as if my four years of absence had been erased.

'And so I was surprised when Baptiste greeted me in the tone of voice and with the turn of phrase reserved for those returning from a long voyage.

'It was Sonia who abruptly separated past from present once more: she had changed...a lot.

'Not that she had aged. I found no trace of wrinkles in her slender face, with its slanting eyes and high cheekbones. It was the look in her eye which surprised me: still simultaneously mysterious and expressive—which is what had captivated me before—but now with something stranger still, something wild. Yes, that's the word: wild.

'"Good evening," she said. "I'm glad that you could come."

'I'd never noticed the softness in her voice, perhaps because she'd never used it before with me.

'She held my hand in hers for slightly too long.

'"Very glad," she repeated. "I needed you to be here."

'I felt very embarrassed by these words, and even more by her tone, because Saint-Luce was watching us. I had the strange fear that he would see in my eyes the echo of her joyful welcome. I hardened my face, sat down slightly farther away and replied with the most banal politeness possible. But Sonia's eyes remained fixed on me and I was unable to adopt a natural attitude.

'At that moment I understood why Saint-Luce had sacrificed his life of adventure for her.

'Happily, the arrival of Gustave Aranc put an end to the awkward situation. He'd reached the castle an hour before us and planned to stay as long as necessary.

'Was it at that moment that I began to dislike Saint-Luce's nephew? Or did I retroactively assign my later feelings to that first encounter? Probably the latter, for there was nothing to justify such antipathy at the time.

'Aranc resembled his uncle, tall like him and with the same sharp features. The only difference was that he was blond, not brown-haired, which created a contradictory impression: he appeared less energetic than Saint-Luce—the Saint-Luce of yore, that is—but his eyes appeared harder.

'He was very young-looking: one would not even have accorded him his proper age: twenty-six.

'His welcome was cold but correct.

'It was after dinner that he began to displease me. I had, quite naturally, started to talk to him about his adventures in Africa and mine in India. It was a subject which should have drawn us together as fellow hunters.

'That wasn't how it turned out. He responded, not coldly, but with indifference. I found none of the juvenile enthusiasm I expected.

'I soon worked out the reason. It was not me he wished to talk to, but Sonia. He was sitting close to her and interspersing his replies to me with comments to her made in a low voice. The effect was to cut both Saint-Luce and me out of their conversation, no matter how banal. My old friend and I finished up by withdrawing to a spot near the window and talking amongst ourselves, just the two of us.

'Saint-Luce appeared nervous and kept casting an eye in their direction. Knowing him as I did, I anticipated a sudden explosion.

'It didn't happen. And never more than on that evening, did I understand just how much my friend needed help.

'I asked him:

'"What time did it start last night?"

'He realised immediately that I was talking about the howling.

'"Right on the stroke of midnight."

'"Let's wait until then," I suggested.

'How long it took to come! There were periods when we sat for a quarter of an hour without saying anything.

'Eventually, the twelve chimes sounded on the great clock in the hall. My heart stared to beat faster... Minutes passed without incident.

'"I wasn't expecting it tonight," said Saint-Luce. "They want to prolong the agony."

'"So, let's go to bed," I replied, "because nothing's going to happen."

'It wasn't that I was particularly tired. But the *tête-à-tête* between Sonia and Aranc was irritating me—due partly to jealousy, no doubt, but much more to fear of an explosion by Saint-Luce.

'As we stood up he gave me not just a candelabra, but also a small electric pocket-light.

'"We've all got one," he said.

'It seemed like a wise precaution, even though it had also been decided, I noted, to leave one candelabra to light the corridor. The extra-long candles could theoretically last until dawn...but they could also be blown out very easily.'

*****

'I had asked for the same room as before. That was where I had previously heard the howls and I couldn't be sure it would be the same elsewhere.

'For two hours I stayed up, straining to hear something, without success. I went to bed and fell quickly asleep.

'After I don't know how long, I was awoken by the sound of a door closing. Not very violently, normally enough, but the sound reverberated under the vaulted stone ceilings.

'There was nothing unsettling about the noise and I went back to sleep soon afterwards.

'It was not until the next morning that the mystery became apparent.

'I'm an early riser, so I was the first into the dining room, with the hope of finding Baptiste to serve me breakfast.

'But as I approached the candelabra I stopped in surprise. I'm talking, of course, about the one that had been left in the corridor to last until morning.

93

'It was extinguished, *but the candles had only been half consumed.*

'Who had taken the initiative to blow them out during the night? I couldn't imagine who and started to become vaguely uneasy.

'I found Baptiste in the dining room and asked him about the mystery.

'"It wasn't me, monsieur," he replied.

'"Has it ever happened before?"

'"No, monsieur. Since we started doing it a month ago, the candles have always burnt down to the end. Every morning, I extinguish the three or four candles that are still lit."

'He also appeared uneasy and it seemed to me he regarded me with a suspicious eye.

'"I heard a door close last night. Could it have been a gust of wind?"

'"No, monsieur, there's nothing open in the castle—and, in any case, there was no wind last night."

'I ate in silence and went to the library, where Saint-Luce joined me shortly thereafter. By his worried look I saw that he also must have noticed the anomaly. Before he could open his mouth, I anticipated him:

'"Yes, it's bizarre. The candles must have been blown out at around three o'clock in the morning."

'"That's what I think, too."

'"I hope it was either you or Sonia."

'"Of course not. That would have been stupid."

'"I'm aware of that, but one must cling to the faintest hope. It wasn't Baptiste either and I'd be surprised if your nephew would do such a thing."

'"Did you notice anything else?" he asked me.

'"Yes. Oh, nothing to worry about: a door closing."

'"So that wasn't you?"

'"No," I replied. "Perhaps Sonia?"

'"Not her either. She was by my side when the noise woke me up suddenly."

'"Could you assess which direction the sound was coming from?"

'"No, I was asleep, as I told you. One is disoriented when one is suddenly awakened. But there can be no doubt: it was the door of my nephew's room."

"'Why?"

"'The sound must have come from the second floor, there can't be any doubt about that. We wouldn't have heard anything coming from the first floor and Baptiste, whose room is there, didn't hear anything. Now, there are only four of us on the second floor. Consequently...."

"'Yes," I replied without conviction—for I knew that logic would not be of great help to us.

"'Obviously!" declared Saint-Luce, as if he were trying to convince himself.

"'Did you take note of the time?"

"'Yes, it was seven minutes past three."

"'Which is just about the time the candelabra went out."

'Saint-Luce nodded his head thoughtfully. Changing the subject, I made the only positive remark I could think of:

"'By the way, I didn't hear any howls in the night, even from far off."

"'Don't worry," he replied with a sneer. "You'll hear them soon enough and louder than you'd like."

'Gustave Aranc entered the room. When he asked me if I'd slept well, I took the opportunity to ask him, with a smile:

"'As a matter of fact, you woke me up. It's not your fault, the castle is a veritable echo chamber."

"'I woke you up?"

"'Yes, when you closed your door. It's of no consequence, I went back to sleep straight—."

'He cut me off:

"'I didn't leave my room the whole night! I did hear the sound of a door, just as you did, but I didn't pay any attention."

'We three looked at each other in consternation. I was the first to speak:

"'Did either of you notice anything afterwards?"

'No, just like me, they'd gone back to sleep straight away without suspecting anything. Or maybe listened for a minute or two without result.

'The lack of suspicion was easy to explain: the door had been closed so simply and without complication that it appeared completely in the normal course of things.

"'So nothing unusual happened," added Aranc.

95

'He hadn't noticed the state of the candelabra, so I put him in the picture. Then he, too, became anxious: more anxious than we were, it seemed. But at the time I didn't attach any importance to it.'

*****

'During the morning I went for a stroll in the park with Saint-Luce. Baptiste raised the portcullis for us and lowered it again once we were outside. I think I told you it was kept permanently lowered now.

'I decided to speak frankly to my comrade, even at the risk of frightening him further.

'"It seems obvious to me," I told him, "that someone got into the castle last night."

'"Obviously," he replied. "Even though it's impossible."

'"Are you absolutely sure?"

'"Take a look!"

'He pointed to the castle, which had no other entry than through the portcullis. The only apertures in the ground floor and first floor walls were the arrow slits, through which not even a child could have passed. All the windows on the second floor were shut tight and the exterior steel shutters were firmly in place.

'One might argue theoretically that someone from the inside could have opened a window for the visitor. But the height of the windows—as you can see from the photo, monsieur—rule that out. The windows themselves are ten metres above ground level and, because of the depth of the moats, one would need a ladder of twice that length to reach them. Not to mention that the slippery mud at the bottom of the moats would have made it nearly impossible to anchor such a ladder.

'I did think about the little door I told you about at the beginning, which opened directly onto the moat, just above water level. In fact, just before we'd gone out, I'd checked it again and determined it was absolutely unusable. And Saint-Luce confirmed as much.

'Then I had another idea. I remembered how Carlovitch, several years earlier, had managed to escape. As you will recall, he'd simply placed a block of stone under the portcullis to prevent it from being lowered completely. Couldn't someone have done the same thing the

96

night before?

'Saint-Luce, on hearing this, shrugged his shoulders.

'"Don't you remember," he said, "that it was lowered yesterday, immediately after our arrival? I even waited for it to be done before we went upstairs, and you saw it yourself."

'"True enough."

'"And nobody raised it after that, or we would have heard, because it's very noisy. What's more, before I went to bed I took the precaution of going down to check, in the company of my nephew and Baptiste. Everything was normal."

'My eyes scoured the facade.

'"You can keep looking as long as you like," continued Saint-Luce. "There's not the slightest fissure, at the front or at the back. As for the arrow slits, only a cat could get through."

'"A cat or a monkey," I agreed distractedly.

'We continued our walk. I declared suddenly:

'"There must be an underground passage!"

'"No."

'"Are you sure? In these old castles——."

'"Absolutely certain. My grandfather had them all walled up because they were crumbling and it was dangerous to go there."

'"And what happened to the external exits?"

'"They've all collapsed. There was no longer any advantage in having them, because they'd become too visible as the surrounding forests disappeared and gave way to moorland."

'"Are you sure?"

'"My grandfather traced them meticulously and blocked them as well. Over three hundred years, as you can well imagine, all traces have disappeared."'

*****

Pierre Herry paused in his narration.

'That's why,' he said to M. Allou, 'I said not to consider subterranean passages. If there had been any, Saint-Luce, in the state of panic he was in, would surely have thought of them.'

CHAPTER XIV

THE FOOTPRINT OF THE BEAST

'We were, as I was saying, in the park.

'Suddenly the bell of the park gate started ringing.

'"One of the merchants, no doubt," said Saint-Luce.

'We went over to the gate ourselves, to avoid Baptiste having to raise the portcullis. It was the postman.

'Despite his outwardly calm appearance, Saint-Luce went pale. He was dreading another anonymous letter.

'"Nothing for you, monsieur le Comte," said the man. "But is there a M. Pierre Herry visiting the castle?"

'I was stunned.

'"I am he," I murmured.

'You will understand my reaction, monsieur, when you realise that I had told *nobody* about my visit to Saint-Luce.

'As I held the envelope, my hand stared to shake. I had recognised the handwriting, the same as in the letters my friend had shown me the day before!

'I stared at it without daring to open it. My eyes were drawn to an insignificant detail: my name had been spelt "Herri" instead of "Herry."

'"Read it," said Saint-Luce.

'I broke the seal, pulled out the piece of paper and read:

'"*Monsieur,*

'You are meddling in affairs which do not concern you. Leave the castle before tomorrow evening, or it will be the worse for you."

'Saint-Luce had read it at the same time. His eyes sought mine.

'"He's wasted the postage," I said. "If I'd had any intention of leaving before, this letter would have been enough to make me stay."

'Saint-Luce offered me his hand and shook mine without a word.

99

'At that moment, monsieur, I felt ashamed. For it wasn't because of him that I was staying....

'Nevertheless, I said nothing. That was my first betrayal. And the second, alas! was to follow shortly.'

*****

Pierre Herry had stopped.

'Continue,' said M. Allou.

'I hesitate to reveal what followed. It would be so improper on my part.'

'At this point, monsieur, we're beyond all the rules of polite behaviour,' said the magistrate. 'In other circumstances I wouldn't ask, but you have to tell me everything.'

'You're right. And, besides, the press has already revealed the worst of it.'

'I'm listening.'

*****

'Lunch passed without incident.

'I was beginning to dislike Gustave Aranc more and more. Not only because of his attitude towards Sonia—for on that score I was reassured: I noticed she replied coldly to him and it was me she looked at.

'What I reproached the young man for was something indefinable in his attitude...something feline. He struck me as lacking virility. My impression was born out later, as you will see.

'Now I come to the essential point of that afternoon. I found myself for a moment alone with Sonia in the library. You no doubt recall that in the course of my earlier visit she had shown complete indifference to me. I had been happy, during lunch, to note a change...which was about to accelerate.

'She bade me sit down close to her on one of the settees, where she talked first of her youth, which had been vibrant enough, and then the years of misery with Carlovitch. Her voice, which was capable of great tenderness, was a sort of cooing, but without any blandness, due to a throaty quality in the timbre and in the accent.

'At that moment I understood why so many men had lost their reason over Sonia!

'Then she talked about her fear. That's not quite the word: more like "terror." Sonia, so full of contrasts, possessed one above all others: to be simultaneously cowardly and resolute.

'I had already observed that during the night we were searching for Carlovitch. She had followed us everywhere without showing any faintheartedness, but had screamed with fright when we were about to leave her alone.

'That afternoon she suddenly took both my hands:

'"You'll stay won't you? You'll stay to defend me?"

'"I promise, Sonia."

'"You're the only one I have confidence in."

'"Let's go away together," I said suddenly.

'That, monsieur, was my second betrayal. I couldn't help myself. She had bewitched me.

'"You love me, then?" she murmured.

'"Let's go away," I urged more strongly.

'And I told myself it was pointless for her to expose herself to danger; that, after all, Saint-Luce deserved his punishment and should submit to it alone.

'"Maybe..." she said in a low voice. "Let me think about it...until tonight. Get up! Here he comes."

'And, indeed, I could hear the door close. I quickly sat down on a settee farther away, and Saint-Luce came in.'

*****

'Sonia had promised me a response by that evening. But I sought in vain for an opportunity to be alone with her. Her lover, who had probably become suspicious, never left her for an instant.

'Just as on the night before, we waited until midnight.

'"Nothing's going to happen," said Saint-Luce.

'"Why not?"

'"The letter gave you until tomorrow to leave."

'He was right. Nothing happened and we parted company soon after.

'As I opened the door to my room, my heart missed a beat. There

101

was an envelope on the table. But as I got closer, I realised I didn't recognise the handwriting. I opened it and found it was a letter from Sonia.

'It was taken away from me, monsieur, but I know it by heart:

'"*Pierre, it would not be right to abandon him at this moment. But soon I shall be free. Wait.*"

'It's inexcusable, I know, monsieur, not to have realised the frightful menace the letter contained, for it essentially announced Saint-Luce's imminent death.

'But at the time I only took note of the refusal.

'I had gone over our imminent departure in my mind too often not to feel a terrible disappointment.

'I wrote a reply immediately, without knowing how I would deliver it to her. I was sure I would find a way to slip it to her the next day. It said simply this, for I had not the heart to write more:

'"*Sonia, I want you to come away with me. Nothing else matters. I'm ready to do anything.*"

'And I placed both papers in my wallet.'

*****

'I didn't go to bed.

'I had no desire to sleep, as you can imagine, and I was also consumed with curiosity. Something was going on and I wanted to find out what.

'I blew out the candles and placed my revolver and electric lamp by my side. I monitored the time on the luminous face of my watch. Still on full alert for the slightest noise, I repeated the words of Sonia's letter to myself. My predominant emotion was now astonishment, for if Sonia were so sure of danger, how did she summon the courage to stay? For I knew her to be a coward—a characteristic I can forgive in a woman.

'I couldn't understand. Or, rather, I could see only one explanation: she was more afraid of Saint-Luce than of the mysterious danger. But I rejected this theory, which my self-respect could not admit. It would mean that Sonia judged me incapable of defending her.

'My watch showed two o'clock...and then three. Still no sounds...of mysterious howls, or anything else.

102

'I eventually fell asleep and was awoken by the dawn light. I got up, already joyful: it takes so little, in such circumstances, to rekindle hope. Because one night had passed without event, I felt that all had been saved.

'Alas, hardly had I set foot outside my room when the expression on Baptiste's face brought me down to earth. I could sense that another misfortune had occurred.

'"Come and look, monsieur," he urged in a low voice.

'He had opened the shutters wide and daylight was streaming into the corridor, clearly illuminating everything.

'He led me to the wall and pointed to a spot between two armchairs.

'This time I was truly afraid, monsieur, for I immediately recognised it for what it was: the footprint of a wild animal, there in yellow on the tiled floor!

'Unfortunately, the claws had made no impression on the tiled floor and the paw was not as clear as it would have been in soil, but one could distinguish the base of the toes.

'As an experienced hunter, I couldn't mistake the nature of the footprint—nor, unfortunately, could I identify which animal had left it. In any case, the print was far too large to be that of a cat.

'As far as I could determine it had been formed by sawdust, and I said as much to Baptiste.

'"Yes, monsieur, I left a small pile behind yesterday by mistake, after sweeping up."

'I could see the pile now, on the other side of the armchair. There was a furrow a few centimetres deep across it. It looked as though the creature had leapt over the armchair, brushing the sawdust with one of its paws. There were large spaces between the pieces of furniture.

'"I discovered it while I was sweeping just now," said Baptiste in an expressionless voice.

'This time I didn't make fun of his fear. The discovery was the stuff of nightmares.

'I studied the footprint, trying in vain to identify it. It belonged to a medium-sized carnivore such as a wolf. It was impossible for it to have passed through an arrow slit; to have passed between the bars of the portcullis was unlikely but not impossible. Such animals can squeeze through apertures which seem too narrow for them, as anyone who has seen a panther squeeze through a gap in a fence can confirm.

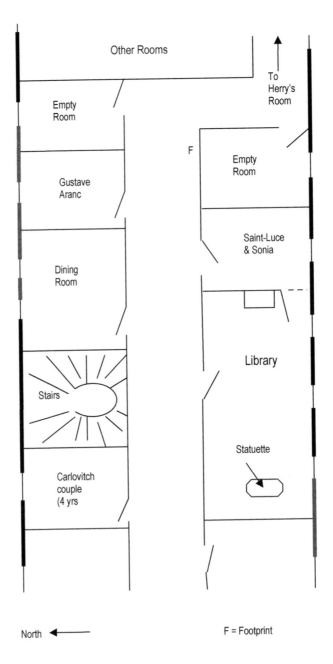

Other Rooms

Empty Room

Gustave Aranc

Dining Room

Stairs

Carlovitch couple (4 yrs

To Herry's Room

F

Empty Room

Saint-Luce & Sonia

Library

Statuette

North

F = Footprint

'"Don't touch anything," I told Baptiste.

'I went for breakfast and was soon joined by Saint-Luce.

'"So nothing happened in the night?" he asked, in a voice more casual than usual.

'He frowned when I didn't answer.

'"Look around the corridors," I said eventually.

'He was back a few minutes later.

'"I didn't notice anything," he declared. "The candles seemed to have burned down normally."

'I realised he hadn't noticed the animal print, which was situated very close to the wall and between two armchairs—as I wouldn't have done, either, if Baptiste hadn't pointed it out.'

*****

M. Allou interrupted:

'So you had, in fact, passed by it once without seeing it?'

'Yes, monsieur.'

'Could you explain the layout of the premises in more detail?'

'Certainly. As you arrive on the second floor from the staircase, you see the door to the library straight in front of you. Looking to your right, you'll see nothing but empty rooms, one of which was occupied by the Carlovitches at one time. Turning left, the door to the dining room is to your immediate left with Gustave Aranc's room adjacent to it. Opposite the dining room, adjacent to the library, is Saint-Luce's room, where Sonia is also staying. From there on, there are no more doors in that section of the corridor, just a couple of armchairs backed against the wall; the footprint was found between them.

'After that, the corridor turns at right angles and then left again, and if you follow the continuation you arrive at my room.

'You can see how, in the morning, making my way to the dining room where Baptiste was, I could walk past the footprint to my left without noticing it until he told me about it and had me retrace my steps.'

'It's all very clear. Pray continue.'

CHAPTER XV

THE BEAST WILL RETURN TONIGHT

'I led Saint-Luce to the footprint.

'He stood there for a long time in silence, seemingly short of breath.

'"I don't recognise it," he said at last.

'A few moments later, he invited me, just as the day before, to walk with him in the park.

'I scoured the ground and so did he. But it hadn't rained for some time and there were no traces to be seen.

'We didn't speak. I noticed he was hovering near the gate and suddenly realised why: he was waiting for the postman.

'Sure enough the fellow soon arrived. Saint-Luce seemed about to greet him at the gate, but gave up and leaned motionless against a tree instead.

'"A letter for you, monsieur le Comte."

'It was I who thrust my hand between the bars to take the envelope. I recognised the handwriting from the day before and, as I looked towards him, he understood.

'"All right," he said. "Give it to me."

'But the hand he extended was lifeless and the letter fell to the ground. I bent down to pick it up and decided to open it myself. I was about to read it out loud, but stopped. It was more terrible than any of the others. It contained only two sentences:

'"*Tonight the beast will return. There will be no more warnings before the third time.*"

'You understand the reason for my reaction, monsieur: "No more warnings"! The letters up to that point, unnerving though they had been, were all reassuring on one point: they promised a delay; one knew there would be further threats before the final execution.

'Now, all that was over. The beast would return that night, we could count on that, but how long before it howled for the third time? An hour? The following night? A week later? There was nothing specific. And I remembered what the last one had said:

107

"When the beast howls for the third time, you will die."

'Saint-Luce finally tore the letter from my hands and read it himself.

'In such cases, monsieur, one says anything to create the illusion of a defence which one senses is impossible. I grabbed Saint-Luce by the shoulders and shook him to get his attention:

'"Are you quite sure that statuette is lost? You wouldn't be trying to hide it secretly?"

'A stupid assumption. One look at his tense features was enough to see that he was desperate. Saint-Luce merely shrugged his shoulders.

'"Then," I exclaimed, "we must leave. This very day!"

'"To go where?"

'"Anywhere! To hide you! Paris, with me, or in a hotel. Or abroad. The world is vast and a man can easily lose himself without trace."

'He shook his head:

'"That's an illusion. You can hide for a few months or even a few years. But when people who are well-organised decide to find you and are prepared to pay what it takes, they will succeed."

'"Well at least you'll have gained a few years...."

'The argument was so wretched it provoked an outburst:

'"Years like that? No, thank you. I would have had to have lost my reason, or hate myself more than my enemies do, to accept that. Can you imagine years spent as I am doing now, jumping at the slightest noise, scrutinising every new face? There's no worse torture."

'"Well at least you'd give yourself a chance to escape," I retorted. "Whereas here you know it's a foregone conclusion that nothing can save you."

'He calmed down a little and continued in a subdued voice:

'"Here, at least, I know the lay of the land, the faces. And, above all I know at what moment the danger will arrive; as soon as the beast has howled for the third time. The arrival of the enemy will be a matter of seconds, minutes or hours at most. I can face them standing, not in an ambush. And if I am to win, my greatest chance is here, where I can look the enemy in the face. At that moment, I assure you, I shall no longer be afraid!"

'What could I say, monsieur? Many times since then I have reproached myself for not insisting. And I've searched my

108

conscience, bitterly. Was my silence out of loyalty, or was I subconsciously hoping for the death of my comrade and for Sonia to be free?

'Yet I don't think so. I believe that it was out of loyalty to Saint-Luce that I didn't insist: that he had indeed convinced me. Wasn't he inside a castle, after all, with the best conditions for taking a stand? What's your opinion, monsieur?'

'I haven't got one,' replied M. Allou. 'Continue.'

'We went back inside in silence. The creaky portcullis rose and fell to let us pass.

'I had taken my letter to Sonia out of my wallet and placed it in my jacket pocket, ready to hand it to her whenever the opportunity arose. The danger was getting closer. Wasn't it, in all conscience, my duty to get her out of there? I still believe so, today.

'But the opportunity never presented itself. Saint-Luce seemed to fear solitude, for he never left my side.

'Lunchtime arrived. The meal was even more gloomy than normal. I didn't try to liven things up. Sonia didn't look at me; her eyes were slits of green. Gustave Aranc must have sensed something, for he remained quiet as well.

'Nevertheless it was he who was the first to react. He suddenly banged his fist on the table and snapped at Saint-Luce:

'"Well, say something, dammit! Have you received a new threat?"

'Saint-Luce took the letter out of his pocket. He waited until Baptiste, who had just come in, finished clearing the table. As the servant was about to leave the room, he suddenly said:

'"You need to hear this as well, Baptiste. I haven't the right to expose you to danger without your knowledge. After you've heard this, you can make your own mind up and I won't reproach you for it."

'He unfolded the letter and read it out aloud. No one said a word.

'"You may leave today, Baptiste," he continued. "You have my permission."

'I looked at the man. I knew he wasn't brave. I told you how he'd abandoned his master in India. But I also knew his loyalty. His internal struggle was only too evident: cold fear versus generations of loyal service. He opened his mouth to speak. At first nothing came out, but I eventually heard:

109

'"I'll stay, monsieur le Comte,"

'Saint-Luce got up and, without a word, went over to shake his hand.

'"By Jove!" exclaimed Aranc. "Then we'll all stay."

'I had the impression that his voice had been pitched too high and his affirmation was largely theatrical. Was it remorse on my part that made me judge him like that? He claimed to speak for all of us, which I for one could not have done.

'Nonetheless I didn't contradict him, but I did lower my eyes when Saint-Luce looked silently around the table.'

*****

'We went back to the library and had hardly been there five minutes when the cook came in. As I told you, I didn't like her much, and even less so at that moment. Everything about her displeased me, from the furtive look in her eye to her feeble voice, which lacked the courage to be openly cowardly, if you see what I mean.

'"Monsieur le Comte," she murmured, "Baptiste just told me and... and—."

'"And you're afraid?" cut in Saint-Luce with such disdain that she almost looked ashamed.

'"What I mean to say is... monsieur le Comte will understand that... at my age... a woman...."

'"Leave this afternoon," said her master curtly, turning his back on her.

'She retreated backwards out of the room, with vague nods of her head to which only Aranc responded amiably.

'I was somewhat surprised by his gesture, but even more so by what he did next.

'I was sitting with Saint-Luce near the window. Aranc, as on the previous day, had gone over to sit next to Sonia on the settee... and, bit by bit, his behaviour became stranger and stranger.

'Even though she didn't respond to him, he spoke insistently to her in a low voice. Each time he attempted to get closer to her she edged further away, but he simply repeated the process.

'None of which escaped Saint-Luce. Little by little I could see his regard change, from a fixed stare to a hard look to one more

110

menacing.

'Aranc must have noticed, but he continued anyway. Soon Sonia was at the very edge of the settee. The young man pushed up against her and bent his head as if he were about to plant a kiss, or so it seemed.

'Was I right? I would never know, because at that very instant Saint-Luce went over and said in a hard voice:

'"Are you going to stop this ridiculous performance?"

'Gustave Aranc stood up slowly and replied calmly and aggressively:

'"Aren't I a little old to be given lessons?"

'"I'll do as I please in my own home."

'"Well, excuse me," replied Aranc. "I didn't ask for your hospitality. It was you who begged me to come here to defend you."

'I could see from Saint-Luce's hands that he was about to strangle his nephew. I made a move towards them but then Sonia spoke in that singing voice of hers:

'"Robert, he's your guest."

'The words stopped Saint-Luce in his tracks.

'"Leave," he hissed at Aranc.

'Strange to say, it was that single word which suddenly clarified the situation for me. I realised that Aranc's whole performance had been aimed at provoking that order.

'I told you there was something about the young man that made me uneasy, but which I couldn't put a finger on. Now I knew: Gustave Aranc was a coward!

'Ever since he'd learnt the contents of the letter, he'd wanted to leave. But that's an awkward thing to do in front of a woman. So he'd found a way to get himself thrown out—and in a manner which could give him the appearance of being courageous.

'Only the appearance, though, because he wasn't genuinely afraid of Saint-Luce. I was there and he knew I wouldn't allow him to be strangled before my eyes.'

'Are you sure you could have overcome your friend?' interrupted M. Allou. 'He was bigger than you, according to your description, and therefore probably stronger.'

'That's true,' replied Pierre Herry.

'So maybe his nephew was less of a coward than you thought?'

111

'Saint-Luce wasn't so much stronger than me that he could have fought off both his nephew and myself. No, I can assure you Aranc wasn't in any danger.

'As soon as I realised Aranc's game I made my own mind up: I was staying!

'My decision was made on the spur of the moment. I didn't think of Sonia or the danger she might be in. It was a purely masculine reflex borne of pride and dignity, beside which women didn't count. Was I wrong? Was I just being an egotistic male? It doesn't matter: I couldn't have acted otherwise—it was beyond my moral conscience.

'"I'm leaving," replied Aranc.

'"You'll be able to share the cook's taxi," I shot at him, like a slap in the face.

'He didn't reply, monsieur, so you can see I was right.'

CHAPTER XVI

THE BEAST HOWLS

'You can imagine what that day was like, monsieur. There was nothing to do but wait for nightfall, which is a greater strain on the nerves than the danger itself.

'I knew something terrible would happen in a few hours and, strange as it may seem, I awaited the moment impatiently. If you've been in the war, monsieur, and sat through the bombardments before the enemy attack, you'll know what I mean.

'Baptiste prepared a nondescript meal. And after we'd finished and were standing up to leave, he gave his master an enquiring look.

'"Come with us," said Saint-Luce.

'The man followed us into the library and, on a signal, sat down apart from the rest of us. Such a presence out of the ordinary underlined the agonising nature of the watch. And it served to remind us that the rest of the castle: its immense rooms, its numerous floors, its distant towers...all that was empty now and there was not a single human being— besides those in the library—who could help us or even hear us.

'A sealed castle isn't a shelter, it's a prison.

'"Search everywhere!" I ordered suddenly.

'I'd said that partly because of the eerie feeling which emanated from the great silent rooms, but also to have something to do instead of the exasperating inaction.

'We must all have felt the same way because, by tacit agreement, our tour of the premises was careful and very slow.

'But eventually we had to return to the library and when we did I checked the clock: ten to eleven.

'The last time we'd finished searching the castle the clock had shown midnight. Why had I thought it would show the same time now? The desire for predictability, no doubt.

'I picked up a book. I didn't feel like reading, but I thought the others would imitate me, which would help us get through the silence.

113

'And, indeed, Saint-Luce and Sonia each picked up a magazine and started turning the pages. Baptiste himself worked up the courage to pick up an old newspaper from the table. From time to time each of us looked at the clock, but furtively, as if to hide our anxiety from the three others.

'At last it was midnight. Nobody pretended to read any more, and all heads looked up.

'Suddenly we were all on our feet. Outside, the beast howled...

'I seem to recall it was quite brief, but I can't be sure.... Something horrible: a sneer, a moan and howl, all rolled into one.

'In the park? On the other side of the wall? Impossible to say.

'I was the first to speak, once the silence had returned:

'"It's not quite the same."

'I was referring, as you will have guessed, to the sounds I'd heard four years earlier, the memory of which remains clear in my mind.

'"No, not quite the same," agreed Saint-Luce.

'"At the time," I said, "I would have sworn it was an animal. Now I'm not nearly so sure."

'"In any case," declared Saint-Luce, "I never heard such a howl in Africa or India. It's like a hyena, but there's also something...."

'I hesitated before I added succinctly:

'"Something more human?"

'"Yes," he murmured. "Yes."

'I've never heard a hyena, having never hunted in Africa; if I'd given that impression, it's because the howl did, in fact, seem more human than animal to me.

'The other one—during my previous stay—didn't have the same character. It's true that I only heard it from afar: would it have sounded different if it had been closer?

'Several minutes had passed, during which Saint-Luce and I exchanged *sotto voce* remarks. Did Sonia overhear us? I don't know. She had remained standing stock still, clutching the back of one of the armchairs.

'Suddenly she fell backwards before anyone could make a move to stop her. She had fainted.

'Saint-Luce and I picked her up and placed her on the settee. I turned round to ask Baptiste for help and realised straight away I couldn't count on it. The poor fellow was looking at us without

114

seeing, not trying to understand, and blind with terror.

'We were able to revive Sonia reasonably quickly.

'"What are we going to do now?" she asked.

'I had thought myself to be calm and collected, but the question left me speechless, unable to form any response. Was the danger past? Should we try to sleep to conserve our forces? Or were the howls— the third!—going to start again soon?

'"I don't know. I don't know," I babbled.

'Never before had I given such a response in the face of danger. My decisions had always been immediate and instinctive, preceding even thought. You mustn't judge me, monsieur, on my present state. Today I am another man...a shadow of my former self. And it was then and there that it began.

'Saint-Luce answered in my stead:

'"Watch," he said, simply. "You, Sonia, lie down on the settee and get some sleep. The rest of us will take turns."

'It was the right way to conserve our resources, but, as you can imagine, nobody felt like dozing off until the morning.

'Dawn always brings in its wake a feeling of peace—inexplicable in our case because the danger remained the same. Nevertheless, when the first rays of light appeared, I fell into a deep sleep.

'I was awoken from my slumber by the grinding of the portcullis. I automatically checked the time: nine o'clock.

'Looking around the room, I could see that Saint-Luce was still asleep. He opened his eyes when he heard the noise, but closed them again. No doubt he assumed Baptiste was taking care of a merchant, and in his sleepy state had forgotten that the cook was no longer there. So, if Baptiste were to go to the front gate, there would be no one to lower the portcullis behind him.

'I got up at once to take care of it and it was only then that I noticed Sonia was no longer on the settee.

'I went down to the first floor, where I heard the noise of the portcullis being lowered. It was operated from Baptiste's room, you will recall.

'I went in and the servant was there.

'"For whom did you open it?" I asked.

'"For Madame."

'I looked through the arrow slit and saw Sonia in the park, walking

115

away from the castle.

'"Where's she going?" I asked.

'"I don't know. She appeared to be walking in her sleep. She ordered me to open it."

'"You shouldn't have done that!" I exclaimed. "Open it again immediately, so I may go after her.'"

*****

'I caught up with her quickly.

'"Where are you going?" I asked.

'"I don't know.... I'm leaving...I'm leaving here."

'"You want to go? You're right. Leave now."

'But she shook her head.

'"No...I can't abandon him.... He's been so good to me... It would be wrong."

'I didn't dare insist, for it was my view as well. And what bitter regrets I've had since. What use is it staying on a sinking ship?

'But what gave me such absurd confidence is that she hadn't been threatened. No letter such as I had received telling me to leave. She seemed not to be part of the adventure.

'When I'd suggested she leave the night before, I'd been planning to go with her. Now I'd decided to stay, I couldn't see any reason for her to leave.

'"Where are you going?" I asked again.

'"I need to get out...get out for a moment...talk to other people. Otherwise I shall go mad!"

'I thought she was right. Her words and her gestures were already becoming increasingly incoherent.

'"Go ahead," I said, "if you think it will do you some good. Would you like me to accompany you?"

'"Oh, no! Don't leave him alone!"

'In her thoughts, as in mine, Baptiste didn't count.

'And so I left her and returned to the castle.

'The new operation of the portcullis—caused by my return and the third in a short space of time—had intrigued Saint-Luce and I found him waiting for me on the stairs.

'"Who went out?" he asked.

116

'I repeated what Sonia had told me.

'"And you didn't stay with her?" he exclaimed.

'"No. She didn't want you to be left alone."

'"How thoughtful!"

'His voice was mocking and bitter. He noticed my expression of surprise.

'"Don't you understand? She's gone to join Gustave!"

'"You're crazier than she is. Didn't you see how she treated him?" I replied, indignantly.

'"Because I was there! Gustave wouldn't have acted like that without prior encouragement."

'I tried in vain to explain my theory about his nephew's conduct, but my words fell on deaf ears.

'"Let's find her," he said brusquely. "Then we'll see."

'We went out into the park and over to the old iron gate which, as you know, was out of order. But the bolts in the little door had been drawn back: Sonia had therefore gone out onto the moor.

'We went out in turn, following the walls of the park and scouring the horizon. It wasn't long before we spotted Père Antoine with his flock, talking to Sonia.

'"You see," I said to Saint-Luce.

'He nodded his head, his features calmer now. Then, without a word, he walked slowly over to the shepherd. It seemed as though he, too, needed the comfort of someone from the outside.

'The large black dog barked as he saw us coming. Or, rather, it tried to bark... And the sight of that great open mouth, from which no sound came forth, troubled me just as before. It was something purely physical, you understand, because now there was no reason to be troubled. Since the howls had become much louder and more intense, it was inconceivable they could have come from that gullet.

'The shepherd greeted us silently. He looked sombre and uneasy. After a moment, Saint-Luce decided to speak:

'"Did you hear it, Père Antoine?"

'"Yes, monsieur le Comte. At forty minutes past midnight. I looked at my watch. It lasted less than thirty seconds."

'Another silence, then Saint-Luce asked:

'"What do you think?"

'"I'm afraid, monsieur le Comte."

'"You were indoors?"

'"Oh, yes! I don't go out on the moor at night anymore."

'"And the dog?" I asked.

'"He went wild, jumping at the door and baring his fangs. If he could have barked, you would have heard it in the castle."

'"Let's go back in," said Saint-Luce.

'He offered his arm to Sonia, who had difficulty walking. I let them go ahead of me. When they were several metres away, I turned to the shepherd, who had his eyes fixed on the departing couple.

'"The next time you hear it," I said, "let the dog loose."'

CHAPTER XVII

THE THIRD TIME

'I only have a vague memory of that afternoon, monsieur, even though it only happened four days ago... but I do seem to recall sleeping for a few hours.

'That evening, after dinner, we were all in the library: Sonia, Saint-Luce, Baptiste and I. I wanted us to talk.

'"It won't be tonight," I asserted. "There's always been a gap between the threats."

'Only Baptiste agreed:

'"Of course, monsieur, of course."

'For he himself found the delay reassuring. He didn't want to look ahead. As far as the others—and I—were concerned, it was a poor consolation: they and I wanted the nightmare to come to an end as soon as possible.

'I abandoned the subject, but, not wishing us to plunge us into silence again, I started my investigation into the events of the day for what seemed like the tenth time:

'"Are you quite sure, Baptiste, that there were no suspicious footprints inside the castle?"

'"None, monsieur, I looked absolutely everywhere."

'What else could I ask him? If the castle was properly sealed? We'd been through it with a fine-tooth comb together, just like the day before, and left candelabras everywhere. The portcullis was down; the iron shutters on the second floor were closed; the enormous bolts which isolated the other buildings from the living quarters were drawn shut as usual.'

'Had you visited the uninhabited parts of the castle?' asked M. Allou,

'No, it wasn't necessary because the bolts were on our side. I can assure you, monsieur, that no human being could have got in. Even though I may have lost my reason afterwards (who can tell?), at that particular moment I was in possession of all my faculties. I *know* that no one could have got in. If there were the slightest doubt about it, the slightest lapse of memory, that would be an immense relief for me. I would clutch at it, monsieur, because it would prove I wasn't mad after all!'

'Do you think you are?' asked M. Allou.

'No! No! I don't believe so. But you, tell me frankly, what's your opinion?'

'You've told me many surprising things, but I haven't detected anything unbalanced in your description of events. On the contrary, you appear very precise and logical.'

'Do I? Well, the things I'm about to describe aren't just astonishing, they're impossible. Do you hear me, impossible!'

Once again, M. Allou examined the tanned face with the sharp features which exuded energy. There was apprehension in those black eyes, but not fear. Did it come from lies which were about to be told and not believed? Or the unlikelihood of facts reported in good faith?

M. Allou hated to jump to conclusions. His gaze wandered to the farthest point in the room as he said, simply:

'Continue.'

'This time, monsieur, I can't give you the precise time at which the thing happened. I didn't look at the clock until afterwards, maybe as much as ten minutes later, at five minutes past midnight.

'It was just like the previous night, meaning it was the same kind of howl, but it had a more tragic significance. The beast had now howled for the third time.

'A hoarse sound behind me caused me to turn round. It was Baptiste, who was groaning and seemed on the point of choking.

'Saint-Luce looked at him. What help could he give the poor fellow? None, apparently, he was simply paralysed by fear. It would be cruel to draw attention to him.

'Saint-Luce went over and put his hand on the man's shoulder.

'"You've been a good and faithful servant, Baptiste, and I thank you for it. You can do nothing more here. Leave us."

'I had the impression the fellow wanted to protest but couldn't find the strength. Very gently, his master nudged him towards the door and he acquiesced.

'"Lock yourself in your room," continued Saint-Luce. "Shoot the bolts. And don't come out until tomorrow. Goodnight, my poor fellow."

'He shook Baptiste's hand, opened the door and, gently but firmly, pushed him out of the room.

'He turned round to face us.

'"Sonia, go to our room. Herry will stay with you."

'"No!" she replied firmly. "I'm afraid, but I'm not a coward. I'm staying with you to the end."

'"I have no right to expose anyone to danger. I alone must pay for the sin I've committed. Leave, my friends. I can defend myself."

'So saying, he pulled out his revolver.

'Over the preceding days, monsieur, I had often seen him distraught and even frightened, unaccustomed as he was to dealing with vague, remote dangers. But, faced with imminent peril, I observed the Saint-Luce of old. His *sang-froid* at that moment was absolute: as if he were face-to-face with a tiger.

'"No!" repeated Sonia.

'"As for me," I added. "You'll have to eject me by force."

'"You're right," he replied.'

*****

'The splendid calmness he displayed dispelled any trace of fear I might have had. I was determined to be as calm as he.

'"Let's take our final precautions," I said. "Let's make sure no corner of this room is in darkness."

'The number of candelabra had, in fact, been increased. At my suggestion, pointless though it may have been, each of us scoured the library thoroughly.

'I think I was the first to cry out, although I think we all saw it simultaneously. On the table at the far end of the room the statuette had miraculously reappeared, exactly where it had been before!'

'At that very instant?' asked M. Allou.

'Ah! That was the question we were all asking ourselves, and nobody knew the answer. There were a considerable number of objects on the table and, as you know, one has a tendency not to pay much attention. The library was a very long room and one's eyes generally didn't wander there.'

'Not even during your previous thorough search?'

'There wasn't a single piece of furniture in the room which could have concealed anyone. We didn't really look at the table, and the statuette was pretty small, as I told you. I can tell you, though, that it wasn't there in the early afternoon, nor even at five o'clock because Baptiste would have noticed as he set out the candelabras. I can't tell you any more than that.

'We looked at it in silence for a while. Then Saint-Luce went over and picked it up.

'"It's the real thing," he announced. "It has come back too late to hand it over."

'"Isn't there a message next to it or underneath?" I asked.

'Any indication about the danger we were in would have relieved my tension. But, alas, there was nothing, and the silence was more menacing than any of the letters had been.'

'Had the portcullis been raised during the afternoon?' asked M. Allou.

'No.'

'Are you sure?'

'Absolutely. Sonia had asked to go outside again, claiming the walls were suffocating her. She had wanted us to accompany her on the moors. Saint-Luce had refused.

'"I'm not leaving the castle any more," he had said.

'So I can confirm the portcullis had not been raised that afternoon.'

'And was the library unoccupied at any time?' asked the magistrate.

'Why, yes. I was in my room and had even slept for a few hours. Saint-Luce was in his.... Certainly the room had been empty several times before dinner. But I can't be more precise than that.'

'Continue.'

'We all looked at the statuette Saint-Luce was holding. He eventually put it down and came towards us. He tried to make light of the situation:

'"This doesn't look too good," he said.

'But the tone of his voice betrayed him and made the irony seem forced.

'Once again, I tried to dispel the dread by giving precise orders.

'"First we must lock the doors."

'There were two: one was the door onto the corridor and the other was the connecting door to Saint-Luce's room. They were furnished with enormous bolts, which I shot.

'You need to understand the positions of the doors, monsieur. The communicating door is at the end of the room farthest from the table where the statuette was standing. It's right next to one of the three south-facing windows in the room—which is the first to catch the dawn light from the east—and perpendicular to it.

'The door onto the corridor faces north. Hence when you leave by one door you can't see the other, unless you turn your head.

'As I was saying, I bolted both the doors.

'"Are the revolvers at the ready?" I asked, taking mine out and checking it.

'"Yes," said Saint-Luce, doing the same thing.

'"And you, madame," I added, turning to Sonia, "are you armed?"

'"No, but I wouldn't know how to use one, in any case."

'"Take one anyway," said Saint-Luce, pulling a second revolver out of his pocket.

'And he showed her how to use it.

'I looked all around: the well-lit room, the shutters closed, the bolts in place... Really, the idea of any danger seemed absurd. And yet, monsieur, I was sure the threat would be carried out.

'But how? That was the question which preoccupied me more than the danger itself. Uncertainty is a terrible torture for the nerves... And it lasted for an hour and a half! You cannot imagine....

'Suddenly I heard a noise, a light but clear metallic sound coming from the adjacent room, Sonia and Saint-Luce's bedroom.

'They heard it as well, because they both tensed, revolvers at the ready.

'Sonia looked at me... And it was that look, monsieur, which was my downfall, and the downfall of us all.

'I loved her, as you know...or, more precisely, I desired her desperately. A man must never behave like a coward in front of a woman, even one to whom he is indifferent. And if he desires her, he is capable of any madness.

'What did we have to fear by staying in the library? Nothing, locked in as we were. But that look, which begged me and filled me with confidence, caused me to lose my senses. I wanted to show myself worthy of such esteem and confront the danger, rather than waiting for the end like cattle in an *abattoir*.

123

'I rushed over to the connecting door and drew back the bolt.

'Saint-Luce started to follow, but Sonia clung to him screaming:

'"Don't leave me alone!"

'She had cried out like that four years earlier, when Carlovitch had disappeared.

'I'd already opened the door and, pulling back the curtain on the other side, had entered the bedroom, revolver in one hand and electric lamp in the other. The lamp was unnecessary, because there were candelabras already illuminating the space.

'The bright light gave me a false sense of security. I had a quick look round and convinced myself there was no one there. The facts were to prove me wrong but, to this day, I still can't convince myself that someone could have evaded my cursory examination. I've hunted in the bush and I have a keen eye.

'Did I lose my *sang-froid*? I think, on the contrary, I was stronger than ever in that moment of danger.

'Be that as it may, and rightly or wrongly—wrongly, no doubt—I crossed the bedroom and opened the door to the corridor, also well-lit. I stood there for several seconds, waiting. To my left the corridor went past the head of the staircase, which was opposite the library door; to the right, it was a short step before it turned in the direction of my own room. I looked both ways and saw nothing.

'And that was when, behind me in the library, I heard the first shot. I rushed back.

'Saint-Luce was lying motionless on the floor, blood pouring from the right side of his forehead. His revolver was still in his hand.

'Sonia was standing a few steps away, leaning on a console. She was wide-eyed, yet appeared to see nothing. Her mouth was wide open as if to scream, but only a whistling sound came out. Her revolver lay at her feet.

'I looked at the door to the corridor, following the direction of Sonia's vacant stare. The bolt was firmly in place, just as I had left it!

'That meant the murderer was still in the room, for I was blocking the only other exit.

'Dropping my electric lamp, I started to turn over the settee, the armchairs, a table and anything which could serve as a hiding-place.

'Unfortunately, I had barely started my search of the huge room when there was a furious knocking at the door to the corridor. It was accompanied by strangled words and I recognised Baptiste's voice. I went over to open the door.

'"The shot...." he began.

'Then he glimpsed his master prostrate on the floor and was unable to finish the sentence.

'As you will recall, monsieur, the head of the staircase was almost opposite the library door. Naturally, I looked over at the staircase, by which someone could have left. It was obviously a stupid thing to do, because the murderer had to be still in the room, but it was a reflex action that everyone would have made.

'At the same time, I asked him a question:

'"Where were you when you heard the shot?"

'"At the foot of the stairs. I'd heard a noise in the room above mine."

'So the murderer had not gone downstairs, or Baptiste would have met him coming up: and he couldn't have passed behind him whilst he was knocking at the door.

'"Call the police," I ordered.

'Baptiste ran quickly down the stairs to the telephone on the first floor.

'All that had only taken a few seconds. I turned to Sonia.

'She was still wearing the same terrified expression, but seemed to have gained more awareness because she gestured towards the bedroom door, which I had left open, and said in her throaty voice:

'"There!"

'I assumed she meant that, in the brief moment that my back was turned whilst I was speaking to Baptiste, the murderer had fled into the bedroom.'

'Wasn't he able to flee before you opened the door to the servant?' interjected M. Allou.

'Impossible. I would have seen him. So, following Sonia's gesture, I ran back into the bedroom. This time I examined it more carefully, but there was no one there.

'But, of course, the door to the corridor was wide open. I hadn't thought to close it when I'd heard the shot, so it would have been easy for the murderer to have left the room that way.

'He couldn't be hiding very far away. He couldn't have taken the stairs because Baptiste was using the telephone on the first floor landing: I could hear his voice.

'Once in the corridor, had he turned left or right? To the left were the stairs, blocked by Baptiste below, and the door to the library, which he was hardly likely to have used, having just got out of that room. Further along there were several empty rooms whose doors I hadn't heard opening.

'Thus I opted for the right, which offered the murderer a safer route because of the bends in the corridor. I ran a few yards in that direction and then stopped dead; a second shot had just rung out behind me!

'It had come from the library once again, of that I was sure!

'At the same time I heard Baptiste on the floor below shouting into the telephone:

'"There's been a second shot. Come quickly or we're all doomed."

'I ran back towards the library. And I had the presence of mind to ask myself, as I ran, which door I should use.

'They had both been left open. I hadn't shut the one to the corridor after talking to Baptiste because I'd rushed to the bedroom following Sonia's gesture. And I hadn't closed the connecting door in my haste to pursue the criminal.

'Whichever one I used now, the murderer would leave by the other. There was only one hope: that I could surprise him by the stealth of my approach. I thought he would more likely leave by the bedroom, since that was the exit he had used up until now. Maybe the logic wasn't impeccable, but in such moments one is guided by one's impressions.

'And this one was, alas, mistaken. Even though I moved in complete silence and nothing could have alerted him, by the time I arrived in the bedroom it was empty; the criminal hadn't passed me on the way; and he wasn't hiding in the room.

'I drew back the curtain and looked into the library. I was so sure of what I would see there that, at the time, I felt drained of all emotion.

'Sonia was lying on the floor, shot in the forehead as well, very close to the spot I'd seen her standing for the last time. She was holding a revolver in her clenched hand.

'I'd noticed that Saint-Luce, too, had been holding his weapon in his hand. Neither of them had had the time to defend themselves.

'Sonia, however, must have seen the danger coming. I remembered quite clearly that while she was clutching the console, her revolver was on the floor next to her. So she must have had the time to bend down and pick it up.

'Or maybe not. Maybe she'd done it before she became aware of the danger....

'By then, monsieur, I was truly afraid. You will recall the threatening letter I received. Sonia, who had received no such letter, had nevertheless been shot. It was blindingly obvious that I would be next.

'It was crazy to be standing there in the middle of the library with both doors of the room open, offering myself as a target.

'I ran across the room to a spot as far away from the doors as possible and crouched down behind an armchair close to the table where the statuette was standing.

'It was a precarious shelter. I told you earlier that there was really no place to hide at that end of the room. The small armchair barely concealed me, but it was better than standing in full view in the middle of the room; and at least I had a wall behind me to prevent an attack from the rear.

'I looked at the door to the corridor, which was slightly ajar, but couldn't see the corridor itself. Then, by raising myself slightly, I tried to make out the door to the bedroom.

'I immediately saw the curtain slightly drawn back and a revolver pointed straight at me.

'I had no time to take action. The shot was fired at that precise moment and I sensed the bullet graze my forehead.

'That's the wound you can see here, monsieur.

'There was no way for me to defend myself. No matter how quickly I brought up my gun he could shoot me three times before I pulled the trigger. I had the reflex of a wounded animal: pretend to be dead so as to pounce on my attacker when he least suspected it.

'Needless to say I'd kept my revolver in my hand. Sprawled out on the floor, I watched out of the corner of my eye, turning my head slightly to avoid being blinded by the blood.

'But I couldn't see anything. It was a sound that caught my attention first: the voice of Baptiste, calling from the corridor:

'"M. Herry! M. Herry! Where are you?"

'It would be his turn next, the poor fellow. He would be killed like the others.

'What should I do? If I responded, it would reveal that I hadn't been mortally wounded and another bullet could be waiting for me. But I couldn't simply abandon him....

'His presence in the corridor gave me temporary protection from that side. I stood up suddenly with my revolver pointing at the curtain, ready to fire at the slightest movement. Then I called out:

'"Baptiste, join me in the library. Use the door in the corridor. Hurry!"

'He came in.

'"Close the door behind you and bolt it," I told him. "Now don't move a muscle."

'With my revolver drawn I edged towards the connecting door. The curtains weren't moving. I reached the door and bolted it.

'"Let's tuck ourselves in the corner by the fireplace," I said. "That way we can't be hit by someone firing through the door."

'Once we were out of the line of fire, I asked:

'"Did you call the police?"

'A stupid question, because I'd heard him. But a need for reassurance caused me to have him confirm it.

'"Yes, monsieur, the police will be here in less than fifteen minutes. They will rescue us. I told them there'd been a second shot. Then I came upstairs and, just as I reached the top, I heard the third shot. You've had a close shave, monsieur. But is it true you saw nothing of the assailant?"

'"Nothing."

'I felt calmer and my courage returned.

'"We need to find out if they're still alive."

'Both bodies were in the line of fire of both doors, but I went over nevertheless. Alas! Both Sonia and Saint-Luce were well and truly dead.'

CHAPTER XVIII

UNLIKELIHOOD

'I went back to the fireplace, trying to piece together what had happened, so I could explain to the police when they arrived.

'I could only see one explanation.

'Sonia, Saint-Luce and I are in the library when we hear a slight noise in the bedroom. It has been made by the murderer, deliberately, to draw our attention to that side of the library and lure us into leaving our shelter and falling into the trap he'd prepared.

'But I'm the only one to leave the library. Because my examination was too cursory, I fail to see him as I cross the bedroom, where he's hiding. Nevertheless, he doesn't fire on me for fear that Saint-Luce, his principal victim, might escape.

'He lets me go past. I go over to the door and look out into the corridor. While my back is turned, he darts into the library and, before anyone can move, shoots Saint-Luce. Then he hides in the same room, training his revolver on the terrified Sonia who dares not make a sound or a gesture... Now alerted, I return to the library.'

'Why,' interjected M. Allou, 'doesn't he just shoot both of you at that moment?'

'Ah, monsieur, you've put your finger on the police's argument. Why doesn't he just kill us then and there? I don't know. I don't understand it myself. The fact remains that mine is the only possible explanation.'

'Please continue.'

'Baptiste knocks on the door. I open it and talk to him. Behind my back, the murderer ducks back into the bedroom again. Following Sonia's gesture I go after him. He's already left the bedroom by the time I enter. However, instead of turning right, as I assume, he turns left and goes back into the library through the corridor door. By the time I've run ten metres or so in the opposite direction, he's fired another shot.'

'Ten metres or so,' said M. Allou, interrupting again.

'That means Sonia would have had time to pick up her revolver, as you said. Why did the murderer wait those few moments?'

'There was no hurry.'

'Excuse me, you could have gone left in the corridor instead of right, for all he knew. In which case, you'd have been right behind him. Why would he expose himself to such a risk?'

'That's true,' murmured Pierre Herry.

'Your explanation doesn't hold water, monsieur.'

'Alas! The investigation proved as much. I offered it because it's the only one.'

'Not so fast,' declared M. Allou.

Pierre Herry stared at him for several seconds in silence, then said, in a low voice:

'I understand. You're accusing me as well.'

'Continue your story.'

*****

'The police arrived a few minutes later. We were alerted by calls from the portcullis. I wasn't surprised they'd reached the castle; I imagined they'd scaled the surrounding wall easily using the shepherd's ladder.

'"You have to go and open it," I told Baptiste, because the portcullis, as you recall, was operated from his room.

'No sooner had I issued the order than I realised its futility: nothing would convince Baptiste to leave the library.

'"I'll go myself," I announced. "Are you armed?"

'"No, monsieur."

'"Bolt the door behind me, you'll have nothing to fear."

'Because I couldn't leave him my revolver, could I? I might need it and he was safe where he was.

'As I left, I looked rapidly left and right along the corridor. Baptiste made things easy for me by slamming the door behind me and cutting off any retreat. My greatest hope of salvation was now my rapidity of movement.

'I bounded to the stairwell, took the stairs three at a time, rushed to Baptiste's room and bolted the door behind me.

'I then went over to the arrow slit and called out to the police to wait there until after the portcullis was lowered behind them, because the murderer was still in the castle. The manoeuvre was carried out accordingly.

'As soon as I heard voices on the stairs, I came out.

'There were a dozen or so inspectors commanded by the same Commissaire Libot as four years earlier.

'He remembered perfectly clearly the lay of the land. Before even listening to my explanations, he verified that the doors leading to the rear parts of the castle were bolted from the inside.

'So the murderer hadn't escaped that way.'

'How do you know that?' interjected M. Allou again. 'Didn't quite a bit of time elapse between the moment you were fired on and Baptiste's first shouts? Couldn't he have shut one of those doors behind the unknown assailant if he were himself an accomplice?'

'No, monsieur, there were only fifteen seconds at most. And the police tested it out. Even for a man far more agile than Baptiste it would take three minutes to go down to the ground floor where those doors are, bolt them and come back upstairs. Remember that the stairs are very long because the floors all have very high ceilings.

'Besides, the rear part of the castle would have been a dead end. And they checked it, just like everywhere else.

'I must tell you, monsieur, that the search was very thorough... Yet they didn't find anyone, even though there must have been someone there. You're not convinced, monsieur, because you suspect me. But I'm certain of it! Either I was raving mad during the several minutes of drama, or someone was there who mysteriously disappeared.

'After the search had been completed, Baptiste and I were interrogated separately.'

'Stop there,' said M. Allou. 'Did you notice anything further yourself?'

'Nothing.'

'I want to hear the details of the investigation.'

'They were devastating for me, I must confess. The material evidence was in complete contradiction to my account and pointed to me as the guilty party. That's what's so frightening about the whole business. Everything I've told you has been barely probable, hasn't it? Well, after the results of the investigation they became impossible, *materially impossible*, no question about it.'

'So?'

'So I don't know. I feel as if I'm living a nightmare. After the discoveries which were made, logic would dictate that I'm guilty. So did I indeed lose my mind during those few minutes? That can happen, I believe, as a result of an intense emotional experience?'

'Yes,' said M. Allou.

'And yet I spoke to you lucidly?'

'Today you did, incontestably.'

'You can familiarise yourself with the investigation through the newspapers. I've collected all of them over the last three days.'

'That won't be sufficient. Wait.'

And M. Allou went over to the telephone.

'Hello, Sallent? It's M. Allou.' Sallent was a commissaire in the Police Judiciaire, whom he had met in the course of a previous case. 'Do you know Commissaire Libot at Versailles?'

'He's an old comrade.'

'Can you do me a favour? I'd like him to come and see me as soon as possible after dinner and tell me all he knows about a case.'

He gave his friend the name of the case and the address where he could be reached and hung up.

He went back into the dining room. Had Pierre Herry waited for him? Yes, he was still there, his head in his hands.

'It's late,' said M. Allou. 'We'll have dinner and you can come to where I'm staying.'

The other hesitated and asked:

'Do you believe me?'

'I'm not the examining magistrate Cordani,' replied M. Allou. 'It's better not to ask me questions.'

CHAPTER XIX

DAMNING PROOF

Commissaire Libot arrived at nine o'clock. He was a small man with a debonair manner, a keen look in his eye and rapid gestures, who gave the impression of having a quick temper.

He found M. Allou alone in the library. Pierre Herry was in the adjacent room with the door ajar.

"You can listen to everything," M. Allou had told him, "but don't show yourself. If there are inaccuracies or imprecisions, you can only correct them after the commissaire has gone, because I don't want to put him in a difficult position. I don't want you arrested here, where you came of your own volition, but he would have to do so if he knew you were here."

Libot, briefed no doubt by his colleague Sallent, wasted no time in getting started. But M. Allou stopped him almost at once.

'What I want from you, commissaire, is only what is known to the general public through newspaper reports. I asked you here purely to get more precision. What I absolutely do not want is for you to reveal secret knowledge unless I specifically request it.'

'That would be very difficult, monsieur le Juge, since there isn't any. The affair, as you will see, is crystal clear with not a shadow of doubt.'

'Please proceed, then. I know all the facts up to your arrival at the castle which, I believe, you have gone through with a fine-tooth comb?'

'You can say that again. We would have found a pin, if that had been the object of our search.'

'And nobody could have got out?'

'Nobody, unless it was with the complicity of the two inhabitants. When the portcullis is raised it makes a terrible racket. And there's no other way out except for a side entrance just above water level which is absolutely unusable.'

'All right, how did you get into the park?'

'We broke down the gate. Our first thought had been to use the old

133

shepherd's ladder which the journalists used four years ago.

'But the sheep farm was empty and we couldn't find the man or the ladder. It was dark, we had urgent business and we didn't want to spend any more time, so we preferred to break down the gate.'

'Fair enough. And then?'

'Then, after I'd searched everywhere I realised I was being made a fool of and the two men became suspects.

'I interrogated Pierre Herry first. He offered me an insane explanation.'

Whereupon Commissaire Libot gave a detailed account which coincided completely with what the magistrate had already heard.

'And furthermore,' continued the commissaire, 'he provided an even crazier explanation, involving moving to and fro between rooms, which didn't hold up under examination. You may have read about it in the newspapers?'

'Yes, indeed. The theory is quite preposterous.'

'It is. I felt certain he was lying and I didn't bother to hide my impression. Incidentally, he'd been mixed up in another fishy business in the same castle four years earlier when a certain Carlovitch disappeared.'

'Excuse me,' said M. Allou, 'but couldn't he have been wrong in his explanation but sincere in his account of it?'

Libot gave him a pitying look.

'Really, monsieur le Juge, it's the kind of thing you read about in boy's comics: miraculous statues, Hindu vengeance and all the rest of it. It just doesn't happen in real life!

'There's only one thing that's real and that's the famous howling of the beast, which everyone heard. But in my opinion, for what it's worth, the whole thing was organised by Herry to make believe the threat came from outside.

'I didn't hide it from him, either. "You're lying," I told him. "You're lying from beginning to end." I grilled him for two hours and several times he appeared about to break down.

'But he didn't. Sometimes he remained silent for minutes on end with his head in his hands. But all he did was affirm stubbornly that everything had happened just as he had said.

'I frisked him, of course. I kept his revolver—or rather, the revolver he was carrying on his person.'

'Why do you make that distinction?' asked M. Allou in surprise.

'You'll understand in a minute, monsieur le Juge. I kept his papers as well. Most were unimportant, but two were of great interest.

'The first, signed Sonia (that's the name of the woman) said:

"Pierre, it would not be right to abandon him at this moment. But soon I shall be free. Wait."

'The second, signed Pierre, said:

"Sonia, I want you to come away with me. Nothing else matters. I'm ready to do anything."

'Now I had the motive, monsieur le Juge, which, frankly I'd suspected all along. *Crime passionel.* The woman refuses to go away with him, so he kills her and her lover. It's as clear as day.'

'Is it really all that clear?' interjected M. Allou. 'Why did she say "soon I shall be free"? Was she anticipating Saint-Luce's death? Did she also believe in the danger from outside? Did she have any reason for believing that?'

'No, it was just a banal formula to keep Pierre Herry hopeful.'

'Curious wording. Why didn't she just say "soon we shall be separated," or something of the sort?'

'It's a detail.'

'Is it a detail that she also says, in the same letter "it would not be right to abandon him *at this moment*"? Why "at this moment"?'

'Because of the anonymous letters which Saint-Luce was receiving. I found them. It's the only true part of Pierre Herry's story.'

'So who sent them?'

'An accomplice, obviously, monsieur le Juge. The culprit tried to pull the wool over Sonia's eyes, to make her believe in an outside attack. He was well aware that, if he were found alone in the castle with his victims, the finger of suspicion would point to him. He believed, naïvely, that we would swallow the story of a ritual crime. It's possible that Sonia believed it, but she's a woman and it's only to be expected.'

'An accomplice in a *crime passionnel*,' murmured M. Allou. 'That doesn't happen very often—.'

'In any case,' interrupted the commissaire, who was becoming irritated, 'it's possible and the rest isn't. The letters, monsieur, constitute the first evidence against Pierre Herry.'

'Is there more?'

'Certainly, and quite damning, as you will see. We have irrefutable material evidence that he's lying.'

'Continue.'

'Not having been able to obtain a confession, I left Pierre Herry in the care of two of my men to await the advent of the examining magistrate who was due to arrive in the course of the morning (it being only six o'clock at that point). And I proceeded to interrogate Baptiste.

'He didn't know very much. His account of his comings and goings coincided with that of Pierre Herry, I must admit. But that doesn't prove anything, because the culprit had constructed his own tale around the servant's movements in the first place. To cut a long story short, I didn't learn anything useful from Baptiste.'

'I read his deposition in the newspapers,' said M. Allou. 'One thing struck me: at the moment the first shot was fired, Baptiste was on the first floor landing instead of his room. Why?'

'But he explained that,' exclaimed the commissaire in surprise. 'He heard a noise like a mechanical click coming from his master's room, which is right above his.'

'Given the thickness of the floor-boards...'

'Oh, I thought about that, monsieur le Juge. And I concluded that the noise came from outside: a stone thrown against an iron shutter.'

'By the accomplice? To what end?'

'The same as always: to make believe in an external attack.'

'That's certainly a possibility.'

'What's more, I found the mark of the stone on the shutter.'

'And not for one moment did you suspect Baptiste?'

'Not as the principal actor, monsieur le Juge. Pierre Herry's account clears him completely. I know Herry lied, but if he'd had the chance to implicate the servant, he'd have done so. The culprit preferred, in his wisdom, not to be contradicted by Baptiste and so he told a story consistent with the servant's movements.

'So, if we accept Pierre Herry's story for the sake of argument, we see that, in the case of the first crime, the door to the corridor was bolted until Baptiste knocked on it. If he'd been the guilty party and he'd stayed behind, hidden in the library, he wouldn't have been able to leave without being seen by Pierre Herry, who had just come in from the bedroom. So Baptiste did indeed come from outside the room, which makes him innocent.

'Regarding the second crime, it's even clearer. Baptiste was telephoning from the first floor landing when the shot was fired; Herry confirms having heard him.'

'So Baptiste couldn't have been anything more than an accomplice, and I can't see how—.'

'One can imagine him helping the culprit to enter and leave by raising the portcullis,' said M. Allou.

'But Herry wouldn't have missed the chance to point that out. Raising and lowering the portcullis can't be done in secret!'

'Maybe Herry had a reason for not pointing a finger at Baptiste, or maybe they both had a reason for not naming the murderer.'

'I can't imagine what that could be.'

'Neither can I.'

'So?'

'So, I said "maybe" and nothing more. We have to examine every possibility, do we not?'

'A reason...a reason...' murmured Libot incredulously.

'Let's just say it was fear and leave it at that.'

'Let's speak even less of it, monsieur le Juge, in light of the following material facts, which contradict your theory. It took me by surprise at first, but it doesn't hold water when I think about it.'

The commissaire's tone was becoming disdainful.

'We'll see. Continue.'

'I frisked Baptiste as well, naturally, but he had nothing of interest on him, not even a weapon.

'Then the examining magistrate arrived, M. Cordani.

'Needless to say we had to raise the portcullis to let him in, but unfortunately we didn't lower it afterwards.

'He interrogated Pierre Herry. There were two of my inspectors behind him, but he seemed so calm and asserted his innocence so clearly that they never dreamed he would try to escape.

'Ah, monsieur, it happened so fast. He suddenly took a fantastic leap forward, displaying a vigour and suppleness quite out of the ordinary.

'He was down the winding staircase in a flash, knocking over the inspector guarding the bridge and reaching the park gate in no time. We'd left our motorcycles resting against the outside of the wall. He grabbed the nearest one—mine, the fastest—and we haven't seen him since.

'He's still on the run.

'But we'll get him. He left his wallet behind, so he has no money. His residence is under close watch. Hunger will cause him to make mistakes.

'Taking flight like that was the second proof of his guilt.'

'Are there more?' asked M. Allou.

'Do you attach such little importance to that?'

'There are those for whom prison is more terrible than hunger.'

'We do have other proof and even better. There was a second search of the castle, more thorough even than the first. In the days following, with the help of an architect we turned everything upside-down, even opening up the old subterranean tunnels, none of which is usable. Not a single hiding-place.

'So Herry lied! Nobody could have got into the castle that night.'

'And during the day?' asked M. Allou.

'I don't understand.'

'Didn't Saint-Luce, Sonia and Herry go out in the morning, and didn't they go out onto the moor to talk to the shepherd. Baptiste was there alone in the castle.'

'That's true, but they searched everywhere again that evening.'

'No, they only searched the south part of the castle, the inhabited part.'

'The doors to the parts behind were bolted.'

'Yes, monsieur le Commissaire, but Baptiste could have bolted one of them behind someone and opened it again later.'

The commissaire shrugged his shoulders and didn't bother to hide his irritation.

'That makes no sense,' he replied insolently. Even if a third party had been involved, the events couldn't have happened the way Pierre Herry described them.'

And Libot explained to M. Allou the objections he himself had

138

raised that afternoon. The culprit would never have acted in the way Herry described: he would have fired earlier, without all the to and fro movement between one room and the other.'

'We agree on that point,' said M. Allou.

'There, you see! Moreover, it wouldn't have been enough for Baptiste to have let the culprit in: he would have had to help him leave by operating the portcullis before we arrived.'

'As I said to you earlier, monsieur le Commissaire, that shouldn't be ruled out, because perhaps Pierre Herry hadn't had the courage to talk about it.'

'He's running a far greater risk by keeping silent about it.'

'If you catch him. Maybe he's more afraid of the criminal than of you.'

'No, that's not possible,' exclaimed the commissaire, who was starting to get angry. 'There were only those four people in the castle. Two of them are dead and the third can't be the guilty party. The conclusion is self-evident.

'Besides, that's not all. I haven't told you about the most damning charge.

'As I told you, we took the revolver Pierre Herry was carrying. We also had the two revolvers from the two victims, which they were each holding in their right hand. We labelled them on the spot before removing them from the scene, so there's no possibility of error.

'When the medical examiner arrived he wasn't able to tell us very much, except the shots had been fired from more than fifty centimetres away, and because of that distance and the positions of the wounds, suicide could be ruled out.

'He removed the bullet from the woman's head. The other bullet had gone through Saint-Luce's skull and we found it embedded in the floorboards. We found a third one in the woodwork.'

'Whereabouts?'

'At the precise spot where Herry claimed to have been wounded.'

'So he didn't lie about that?'

'Oh, monsieur le Juge, there was never any doubt that he was wounded. I saw it with my own eyes. And I'm sure it happened where he said it did. It was after that the lies started.'

'After?'

'What I mean to say is, he knows perfectly well who shot him, and for good reason.'

'Please explain.'

'Very well. We only received the last bit of evidence the following day, after the ballistics report. I'll get to it straight away, and leave the material observations I'd made beforehand until later.

'Listen carefully, monsieur le Juge: what I'm about to say is of paramount importance.

'Two of the bullets, the ones which killed Saint-Luce and Sonia, *were fired from the same weapon*. The one which wounded Herry *was fired from a different weapon!*'

The commissaire stopped to allow the revelation to sink in, savouring its effect, which appeared to be considerable.

M. Allou frowned. There was a thoughtful expression on his face as he slowly filled his pipe.

'From a different weapon,' he murmured eventually. 'So the bullet which wounded Herry was fired from which of the three revolvers?'

Libot paused, leant forward and said slowly:

'From Saint-Luce's.'

'From Saint-Luce's,' repeated M. Allou, nodding his head. 'And which of the weapons was used to kill Sonia and Saint-Luce?'

'Neither Sonia's nor Herry's.'

'But surely you didn't find a fourth?' exclaimed M. Allou.

'We did indeed. I didn't tell you before because you seemed in such a hurry.

'After Herry escaped, we continued to turn the castle upside-down. I didn't think it was really necessary, but I wanted to rule out any possible claims by the culprit.

'So I had the moats drained again. At first sight, once the water had drained off, there was nothing much to be seen—just as I'd expected. Nevertheless I ordered a thorough search, and it was then that I noticed a kind of hole in the sludge, as if a heavy object had fallen in there.

'It was just below one of the library windows.

'The depth of the sludge made things difficult, but we eventually retrieved a fourth revolver!

'There was no rust on it and we surmised it had been down there for less than a day.

'There were two bullets missing from the chamber and it was

quickly confirmed they were the ones which had killed the two victims.

'So you can immediately reach the conclusion—.'

'Just a moment,' said M. Allou. 'Finish the material observations you mentioned first, then we'll look at everything together.'

'The rest is of no great importance. Making a tour of the park wall I came across the body of a large black dog which had been knocked out on the night of the crime and had died.'

'Who did the animal belong to?'

'The neighbouring shepherd. He'd let it out when he heard the mysterious howling.'

'On whose advice?'

'Frankly, monsieur le Juge, I don't know. It could have been his own idea, for all I know. I didn't think to ask.'

'What surprised me most was the reaction of Père Antoine. He cried as if it were a real person. He repeated: "They've killed him. They've killed him," in answer to every one of my questions, as if he'd gone mad.'

'Are you sure he was speaking of the dog?'

'Of course. Who else could it have been? He wouldn't have had the same reaction if it had been the Comte de Saint-Luce, whom he barely knew.'

'So you interrogated him?'

'Vigorously, to put it mildly. You have to understand, I thought he might well have been Pierre Herry's accomplice. He has a reputation for coveting money and might willingly have killed his own dog to make believe in an outside presence.

'So I shook him by the shoulders and shouted: "It was you, you old brigand, who imitated the howling beast; it was you who threw the stone against the iron shutter; if you want to save your own skin you'd better admit it now."

'I couldn't get anything out of him. He just kept shaking his head and shouting, "They've killed him. They've killed him."

'He kept on crying and I began to think that, even to fool us, he wouldn't have killed an animal he loved so much.'

'And the dog?' asked M. Allou.

'But I just explained; he'd been knocked out and had died.'

'I quite understand. What I mean is: did you examine it?'

'Examine it? No, why should I? All dead dogs look the same.'

'And that's all you have to say about the dog?'

'Yes.'

'Did you interrogate any other witnesses, monsieur le Commissaire?'

'Of course. I saw the cook first. She didn't like her master, who frightened her, and Sonia—whom she thought hypocritical and haughty—even less. She didn't bother hiding her feelings, either. A cast-iron alibi for the night of the crime: she'd stayed with friends, one of whom is an inspector in the Sûreté. Nothing interesting to report—her job didn't bring her much into contact with the others.'

'And Saint-Luce's nephew?'

'Gustave Aranc? An even better alibi. When the crimes took place he was in prison.'

'In prison?'

'I'm exaggerating a little, monsieur le Juge; he was detained in a local police station. He was traversing Versailles at one o'clock in the morning at high speed and high volume. He was stopped by an officer and behaved so belligerently that he had to be taken to the nearest station. He appeared to be completely drunk. He was only released the following morning.

'Now the crimes, according to two witnesses and Baptiste's telephone call, occurred at around one forty.

'Aranc, of his own volition, described a scene which had taken place with his uncle, regarding Sonia. Pierre Herry had already told us about it.

'It turns out that Herry had correctly worked out Aranc's motive. He confessed that he'd acted so provocatively with the young woman for the sole purpose of being thrown out of the castle, because he was consumed by fear.'

'Did he also believe the threats of the anonymous letters?'

'Yes, monsieur le Juge. He insisted that ritual vengeance occurs more frequently in Europe than we realise. Maybe amongst savages,' the commissaire added, shrugging his shoulders, 'but they don't follow people to France.'

'Apart from that, did he tell you anything interesting?'

'Nothing. He confirmed what I already knew from the letters: Pierre Herry was trying to persuade Sonia to go away with him.'

'Gustave Aranc knew about that?'

'Yes, Sonia asked him for advice.'

'So they were quite close?'

'In solitary circumstances, monsieur le Juge, one confides in whomsoever one can.'

'Did you find a will?'

'None.'

'So it's Gustave Aranc who inherits?'

'Yes, monsieur le Juge, but I already told you he had a cast-iron alibi.'

'I'm not accusing him.'

'And you can be quite sure that Pierre Herry won't lift a finger to clear his name. He detests Aranc.'

'Once again, monsieur le Commissaire, I'm not accusing him. I'm simply trying to explain his departure....'

'Ah! You're thinking that fear of being disinherited should have prevented him from provoking that scene of jealousy? He must have known what would happen if he abandoned his uncle in a moment of peril, no matter what the pretext, but fear must have overcome self-interest. Once he was resigned to losing the inheritance by abandoning his uncle, he chose the way which would least humiliate him in front of a woman.'

'You haven't understood me, monsieur le Commissaire. My point is that, following his departure, he had every interest in his uncle being killed as soon as possible, before he had time to draw up a new will.'

The commissaire banged his fist on the table in exasperation.

'And I keep telling you his alibi—.'

'That's not the point,' cut in M. Allou calmly. 'I'm simply saying that if, before his departure, he'd noticed something out of the ordinary which foretold danger, he'd kept it from his uncle and done nothing to prevent his death.'

'I don't see what interest....'

'Oh, it's nothing much. It's just that, when he tells you he didn't notice anything, it might be because he daren't say anything now, having kept silent when it would have counted.'

The Commssaire shrugged his shoulders.

'Pure speculation.'

'Maybe, but we mustn't overlook anything.'

'Not even a hypothesis, it would seem. Aranc didn't see anything unusual because there was nothing unusual to see.'

'How do you know that?'

'Because, monsieur le Juge, the ballistics report makes everything clear. What happened is perfectly obvious. I'll explain it if you like.

'Herry waits for the signal from his accomplice—the stone thrown at the shutter in order that Baptiste assumes it's an attack from the outside. It's all part of setting the stage, like the beast howling.

'The he shoots Saint-Luce and asks Sonia to come away with him. She refuses.

'Baptiste arrives just at that moment, Herry gets rid of him by telling him to call the police, and continues his entreaties.

'But Saint-Luce isn't dead. In a last, supreme effort he gets up, weapon in hand, and aims it at his enemy, who has doubtless put his own revolver back in his pocket, thinking to have no further use for it. To defend himself, Herry tries to seek cover by crouching behind an armchair. There isn't enough time and Saint-Luce manages to wound him before finally dying.

'What is your basis for asserting that Saint-Luce didn't die immediately?'

'The medical examiner. He said the victim could have survived for a minute or two, but Sonia died immediately.'

'Fine. Continue.'

'Herry, wounded, implores Sonia one more time. She again refuses. Time is short: Baptiste, alerted by the second gunshot, is on his way back upstairs. She will denounce him. So, as much in anger at being rejected as in fear of being accused, he shoots her. She dies on the spot.

'He throws the revolver out of the window because he knows it can be identified by the bullets. He has another one in his pocket, the one I found on him.

'You see how simple it is, monsieur le Juge? There's no need to rack your brains.'

'Quite,' said M. Allou. 'Even so, to throw the weapon away he would have had to open, not just the window but also the iron shutter, then close them both. That takes time. How much time elapsed, according to Baptiste, between the moment of the third shot and his

144

return to the library? If I'm not mistaken he was on the telephone when he heard the second shot?'

'Yes. He spoke a few more words to notify us of the second shot. Then he went upstairs and had just arrived at the top when he heard the third shot, the one which killed Sonia. He called out and M. Herry shouted at him to enter. Whereupon Baptiste found him in the middle of the room with his revolver pointing towards the bedroom.'

'All very well, but I asked you how much time elapsed between Baptiste's arrival at the top of the stairs and his entry into the room?'

'He told me it was about fifteen seconds.'

'And do you think that was enough time for Herry to open the window and the shutter and then close them both?'

'You can't trust the testimony of a man who's frightened. The time appeared short to him and that's that. If it happens to conflict with the only reasonable theory, then he must have made a mistake.'

'It's a technicality...'

'Look here, monsieur le Juge,' exclaimed Libot, now at the end of his tether, 'if you've another theory which explains everything, then please be good enough to share it with me.'

'I haven't any other than the one I already proposed,' replied M. Allou. 'The escape of the culprit.'

'Then you'll have to excuse me. It's getting late. Is there anything else you wish to ask me?'

'Nothing further.'

'Then goodnight, monsieur le Juge.'

*****

In the street the commissaire, walking with an agitated step, muttered to himself:

'And Sallent told me he was a man of extraordinary intelligence! An imbecile, more likely. A complete imbecile. Good job he's not assigned to Versailles. A fool like that will close his eyes to all the evidence and concoct all kinds of wild theories.'

CHAPTER XX

...

As soon as Libot had closed the door, Pierre Herry came back into the study.

'Thank you for your hospitality, monsieur,' he said. 'You've been a real gentleman. Goodbye.'

'Where are you going?'

'To turn myself in. I would have done so when the commissaire was here, but I wanted to avoid being arrested in your residence.'

'So, are you confessing?'

'No! Everything I told you was sincere, I can assure you. But I heard the commissaire and his theory is irrefutable, unless I accept yours, and I prefer his.'

'Do I have one?' asked M. Allou.

'Yes, you said that I'd let the murderer escape out of fear. I've known fear, monsieur, as has everyone, but I've always vanquished it. I won't allow anyone to accuse me of cowardice.'

'I withdraw my accusation,' replied M. Allou. 'It was a trap I laid for you. If you'd fallen for it, I'd have judged you to be guilty. Because you refused to be saved that way, it doesn't prove you're innocent, but you do merit someone looking into your case for extenuating circumstances, even in spite of yourself. Sit down and let me think. And please don't say anything. I want to make up my own mind.'

*****

M. Allou paced slowly around his study, his hands in his pockets. He had already smoked two pipes and had just lit a third when he stopped in his tracks.

'Where did I put those old newspapers?'

He had in fact, brought them back from the restaurant.

'Here they are,' said Pierre Herry. 'But I went through them all carefully before. After the 21st of October there's not a word about the disappearance of Carlovitch.'

'I'm looking for something else. Let me see, the disappearance was during the night of...'

'The 16th to 17th of October, four years ago.'

'Fine. To be sure, let's look starting from the 18th onwards. But I don't expect to find anything before the 20th or 21st.'

'I've read the earlier papers and there's nothing before the 20th.'

'You don't know what I'm looking for.'

Indeed, it was not the front pages M. Allou was looking at, but the short news items of just a few lines.

When he reached one of the newspapers for the 22nd of October, he read the brief article out loud:

'UNEXPECTED GAME. *In the forest of Meudon, lumberjacks claimed to have heard calls of the wild and spotted strange animals. A beat was organised by local gendarmes and a group of hunters, who shot three superb hyenas which had obviously escaped from a local menagerie.*'

'So?' asked Herry.

'So, monsieur, there is something of interest.'

'I don't see it, particularly since the article is four years old.'

'Wait. Let's look at the next few days to see if the owner of the menagerie was identified... No.... You see, there's no more mention of the event.'

'But what interest...?'

'I know you've never hunted in Africa, monsieur, but you must be aware, like everyone else, of what hyenas feed on....'

'Dead bodies,' murmured Herry.

'Yes, dead bodies. And their jaws are the strongest of all the carnivores. They can grind bones with no effort.'

'You mean...that Carlovitch...'

'Get some sleep, monsieur. I'll start my investigation tomorrow.'

*****

At eight o'clock the next day, Pierre Herry and M. Allou took a taxi to Versailles.

'To the Palais de Justice,' the magistrate told the driver.

Followed by Herry he reached the chambers of M. Cordani, the examining magistrate, and presented his card.

As M. Allou entered, the blue eyes of his colleague expressed nothing but cordiality. But that was replaced by astonishment at the sight of Pierre Herry's profile behind that of the visitor.

'You've...you've arrested him,' babbled the distinguished jurist.

'No. What right would I have? He followed me voluntarily, as you can see.'

M. Cordani was in an embarrassing situation. Should he call the gendarmes for an accused man who had turned up voluntarily? He would look ridiculous. Asking him to go to the prison himself would seem equally grotesque. M. Allou put him out of his misery.

'Arrest him yourself, my dear colleague, as is your duty. But keep him here until midday. You'll find he's very peaceful.'

'Well, that would certainly be one solution. But why midday?'

'Because from now until then, if you agree, we'll work together.'

'By all means, but how?'

'Tell me first about Gustave Aranc's alibi.'

'It's watertight.'

'So I keep being told. A police officer took him into custody at one o'clock in the morning, forty minutes before the crimes.'

'That's correct.'

'Do you have the name of the officer?'

'Yes, the report is in the file. Do you suspect the fellow?'

'No. Just bring him here. I'd like some details.'

Agent Rodie, summoned by telephone, arrived quickly. He had a pleasant and honest face.

He stood to attention.

'Sit down, please. Describe in detail the arrest of Gustave Aranc.'

'Oh, Maître, it was justified.' (He assumed he was speaking to a barrister.)

'I don't doubt it. The vehicle was travelling at a crazy speed?'

'Crazy.'

'And was making a hellish noise?'

149

'Hellish, I can assure you.'

'I believe you, even though I have no reference point.'

'Pardon, Maître?'

'He obviously couldn't have seen you if he continued at such a speed.'

'Oh, Maître, I was right in the middle of the Avenue Saint-Cloud, under an electric lamp. He could see me a kilometre away. I even thought he was going to turn into the Rue du Maréchal Foch to avoid me. He was trying to make a fool of me. He drove straight at me. I made a sign for him to stop and he complied. I approached him and talked to him very politely, as he admits. He responded with such a barrel load of insults that I was obliged to arrest him. I was sure he was drunk and the next day he apologised. But when a member of the public force speaks to you politely, you shouldn't appear rebellious.'

And the officer stopped, seemingly out of breath from his speech.

'You're right,' said M. Allou. 'But didn't it strike you as strange that that a young man in such a rebellious mood should stop immediately at a sign from you?'

The office became red in the face.

'I can't explain it, Maître, but I can assure you it happened just as I said.'

'I believe you. In fact, if Aranc had wanted to get arrested, his behaviour would have been no different, would it?'

'No different.'

'And did you notice anything unusual about his clothes?'

'Nothing. He was very well dressed.'

'That will be all, thank you.'

'But,' interjected M. Cordani, 'are you quite sure it was one o'clock in the morning?'

'One hour and seven minutes, monsieur le Juge.'

'That's not the question,' said M. Allou simply.

His colleague regarded him with astonishment. After the officer had left, M. Allou explained:

'When someone tries to get arrested three quarters of an hour before one of his closest relatives is murdered, isn't one within one's rights to suspect him of establishing an alibi?'

'No doubt, but where's the wrong in that?'

'The wrong, my dear colleague, is in having foreseen the time of the crime!'

'Ah!' murmured M. Cordani. 'You're right....'

*****

'And now,' continued M. Allou, 'let's go to the castle and question the shepherd.'

'We've already done that, and drawn a blank.'

'Then we'll start again. I'll speak to him alone, so as not to frighten him. You can wait nearby, you...and your prisoner.'

M. Cordani looked over apprehensively at Pierre Herry, who was a head taller. But one rarely argued with M. Allou's suggestions. The three men, accompanied by a clerk, climbed into an automobile and, a quarter of an hour later, arrived at the sheep farm.

M. Allou approached alone. Seated on a bench in front of the wall was an old man with a face covered in white hairs. There was a sad, faraway look in his eyes.

'I was a friend of Sonia Carlovitch,' said M. Allou gently.

At the sound of her name the old man's eyes filled with tears. M. Allou sat down next to him and asked:

'Don't you want her to be avenged?'

The shepherd sat up:

'Ah, if I knew the murderer and had him in front of me, these old hands are still capable of strangling him!'

'So why don't you want to help unmask him?'

'Ah!' exclaimed the man in a hoarse voice, 'if you're from the police you can leave. Leave, do you hear?'

His attitude was threatening.

'I'm not from the police. I know they accused you of complicity. I also know it's not true.'

The words calmed the old man, who started to cry profusely, like a child.

'Me, an accomplice in her murder? Ah, monsieur, don't make fun of me. I'm just an old shepherd. All I asked was to look at her when she walked past. And they killed her!'

M. Allou placed a hand on his shoulder:

151

'You can console yourself, Père Antoine, with the fact that she had confidence in you until her dying day.'

'Ah, yes, monsieur, that is indeed a solace to me in my grief.'

'Tell me... It was in the morning, on the moor....'

'Yes...the beast had howled again that night, for the second time... The poor girl was terrified...she had sneaked out to talk to me, which she managed to do before the gentlemen arrived. She wanted to leave, but she said monsieur le Comte wouldn't allow it... He was very hard and cruel... She wanted to leave at night but she was afraid, all alone with the beast roaming... She asked me to come with her as far as Versailles. I was supposed to enter the park at half past one in the morning and throw a stone at her window to signal that I was waiting. I did so, monsieur, after scaling the wall with my ladder... And straight away after that, I heard a shot...and then another...and then a third... I couldn't go inside because the portcullis was down... I stayed there, trembling....'

'Did anyone open the window?'

'No, monsieur, not at that time. Then, later, the police arrived. I hid in the bushes... And I, poor devil that I am, was the first one they accused! I heard M. Herry talking to them, then raising the portcullis to let them in. That's when someone opened a window and a shutter on the second floor and I heard something thrown into the moat. It may have been the revolver they found afterwards.'

'Yes, Père Antoine. Now you have to repeat that to the examining magistrate.'

The old man stood up abruptly:

'No! Never! They'll accuse me, just as before, of imitating the beast's howls. And that's not true.'

'No, Père Antoine, they won't accuse you, I promise. But, tell me, didn't you unleash your dog against the beast that same night?'

'Yes, on the advice of M. Herry, the one they're accusing now.'

'Do you think he's innocent?'

'He was in the castle and it was outside that the dog encountered someone. That only goes to show it was a man who howled, not a beast: the dog was attacked with a cudgel or a hammer.'

'It was a big dog, wasn't it? And because it was mute, and could attack without warning, it wouldn't be surprising to find it had wounded the unknown intruder, would it?'

'It's actually certain that it did, monsieur. There was blood in its mouth.'

'That's what I wanted to know.'

'It gave me great pleasure to see that.'

'No one's going to accuse you of anything, Père Antoine, I promise. But you have to tell the examining magistrate everything. Come with me.'

*****

When the old shepherd had given his deposition and left, M. Cordani was astonished:

'How the devil did you get him to talk? Commissaire Libot, who is energetic and determined, couldn't get anything out of him.'

'Maybe I handled him more gently...and, besides, I knew where I was going. What I was mainly doing was asking him to confirm my theory.'

'You have a theory?'

'Why, yes. But I won't reveal it yet, because we have other people to question. Do you know Baptiste's current address?'

'Yes, he's in a hotel in Versailles.'

'Let's go back to your chambers and summon him urgently from there.'

'What do you want to ask him?'

'Didn't you find it strange, my dear colleague, that in a castle where danger lurked at every turn, this servant who is as fearful as a mouse and is devoted to his master, wasn't armed?'

'Now that you mention it, I do find it bizarre.'

'He's going to have to explain.'

*****

After a short wait, the clerk announced that Baptiste was waiting outside.

'Before calling him in,' said M. Allou, 'arrange for two gendarmes to be posted in the corridor. And also bring in Gustave Aranc, who is a resident of Versailles, as I recall.'

'Two gendarmes...? Ah, for Pierre Herry?'

'Gendarmes are always useful to have around.'

M. Cordani gave the orders by telephone and Baptiste was brought in.

M. Allou stood in front of him and looked him straight in the eye:

'You were seen throwing a revolver out of the window while M. Herry was letting the police in and you were alone in the library.'

'Monsieur, monsieur,' moaned the servant, 'it wasn't mine!'

'Tell us what you know. An accidental wound isn't serious. You would only be fined a few francs, even if charges were pressed. Bearing false witness is something else altogether. If someone is put to death as a result, you will in all likelihood suffer the same fate. It's long past time you told the truth, and this is your absolute last chance.'

'Ah, monsieur, I see that you know everything.'

'Quite so. But tell the story in your own words anyway.'

'Monsieur, I swear I didn't lie during the whole beginning of the story. It was only after....'

'After what?' asked M. Cordani.

'After the two crimes. I was on the telephone when I heard the second shot, the one which killed Madame. Holding my revolver in my hand, I went back upstairs. Needless to say, I didn't dare go directly into the library. I decided to go into the bedroom instead and look into the library by pulling the curtain back slightly.'

'It was brave of you to go back upstairs, all the same,' observed M. Cordani.

'Oh, no, monsieur le Juge. I wanted above all to find M. Herry, so I wouldn't be alone... So, I peeked through the curtain and saw someone crouching behind an armchair...I fired immediately, and it was only while the shot was discharging that I recognised M. Herry! Fortunately, he was only wounded!

'What could I do, messieurs? Tell him I'd only fired on him by mistake? If I did that, he would suspect me of the other two crimes. My behaviour looked suspicious, you understand.

'I didn't say anything...and afterwards it was too late to confess. When the police arrived and M. Herry left me alone while he let them in, he asked me if I was armed. I thought it better to say no.

'While he was raising the portcullis, I realised they would search me and find my weapon. I knew it was possible to identify a weapon if the bullets could be found...they would find out that mine had been fired! So, I had the idea to exchange weapons. I took my master's because he hadn't fired it—not having had the time to defend himself—and left mine in its place.

'The police came in downstairs and I suddenly thought that my precaution was inadequate. I'd told M. Herry that I hadn't got a weapon and nobody would understand why I'd lied. So, while the men were coming upstairs, I opened the window and threw the revolver I'd taken from monsieur le Comte out of the window....'

'You're starting to lie again!' thundered M. Cordani, bringing his fist down on the table with a crash. 'M. de Saint-Luce, as you've admitted yourself, didn't have time to defend himself or use his revolver. Yet it's the one which was recovered from the moat, which you pretend you took from him, which was used to commit the two crimes.'

'But, monsieur....'

'Don't tell me monsieur le Comte committed suicide after killing his mistress, it's scientifically impossible. There wasn't any suicide. So tell us the truth!'

'I've told you the truth! Then we have to believe that someone else before me had the same idea and had already switched revolvers....'

'Aha!' exclaimed M. Cordani, as if he'd had a sudden inspiration.

Pierre Herry stood up, looking very pale.

'And now,' said M. Allou, 'bring in Gustave Aranc!'

*****

'I asked you to come in,' said M. Allou to the young man, 'for a simple piece of information. You spent the two days preceding the crimes in the castle, did you not?'

'No, monsieur. I left at four o'clock in the afternoon on the day preceding the murders—or, more precisely the day before that, for the crimes occurred at one forty in the morning.'

'Where were you on that night?'

'At my residence, where I dined. The servants can confirm it. Then at the theatre, in Paris.'

'Did you go there by motor car?'

'Yes, monsieur. I met some friends there whom I can name.'

'During the intermission or at the end?'

'I don't really remember.'

'We can verify with them.'

'Wait...I remember, it was during the intermission.'

'And afterwards?'

'I went to a bar, where I had a few drinks...more than a few, actually.'

'Alone?'

'With a woman I met there. Then she started to bore me and I left. That's when I had the unfortunate encounter with the police officer. If I'm here about that, I can assure you I regret it and offer my apologies.'

'So you didn't go back to your residence between eight o'clock at night and the time you were released the following morning?'

'No, monsieur.'

'Very well. We can verify all that with the concierge and the servants.'

'Monsieur...wait.... There was a tiny lie in my story. I did return *chez moi* at around half past midnight. That was where I was drinking with the woman, whom I cannot name. I had just taken her back when I met the officer. It was for the woman's sake that I lied. Is it important?'

'Not at all. Another question: since the crime have there been other incidents?'

'Incidents? What kind of incidents?'

'I don't know. I'm asking you. Something disagreeable that one doesn't readily forget.'

'No, absolutely nothing.'

'Absolutely? Are you sure?'

'Very sure.'

M. Allou stood up and ordered, in a terse voice:

'Take your clothes off.'

'Excuse me?'

'Don't you understand? Take off your jacket and your shirt.'

'But why?'

'Do I have to call the gendarmes? Hurry up.'

Aranc obeyed, his face distraught. As he did so, a bandage appeared on his forearm.

'What's that?'

'A dog bit me.'

'Where and when?'

Suddenly the man put his hands together, his face disfigured by fear. He cried out:

'I didn't kill! I swear I didn't kill.'

'So, talk. It was Père Antoine's dog at midnight by the park walls, wasn't it?'

'Yes, monsieur. But I didn't kill!'

'So, who did?' interjected M. Cordani brutally.

'But I don't know...I don't understand anything...you know I wasn't there. I was in prison.'

'Tell us everything you know,' ordered M. Allou. 'Tell us, or we'll charge you with the crimes. You know a great deal and it goes back a long way.'

*****

'A very long way,' admitted Aranc. 'But I only learnt about it a few months ago, from Sonia.'

Whilst he was putting his clothes back on, he began to talk:

'You don't know my uncle.... Capable of anything when he wanted something...

'He'd known and loved Sonia as a young woman. But she had preferred the engineer Carlovitch, whom she adored. Why he hadn't killed the fellow is something I ask myself to this day.

'He went away on big game hunts in India and Africa. That was where he received, four years later, news of Sonia. She was living in extreme misery. My uncle, a major company shareholder, could have found a position for the husband. He was implored to do it.

'Sonia, so as not to irritate Saint-Luce, talked about Carlovitch with a certain coldness in her letter. My uncle began to hope once again— wrongly because the woman's feelings hadn't changed. He had hoped, no doubt, to take her from her husband. But Carlovitch, hypocrite and coward though he was, was still capable of vengeance. It would be preferable to eliminate him.

'In such cases, my uncle scarcely hesitated: the life of a man was of little importance to him. It was then, Sonia revealed to me, that the hideous plan formed in his mind. On his return to France, he would invite the couple to the castle on the false promise of finding a position for the husband, whom he actually planned to kill there, with no witnesses and no risk.

'There was only one problem: if anyone became suspicious about the disappearance, there could be a search of the premises. What to do with the corpse? The biggest problem after murdering someone is getting rid of the body. In the desert it's easy: they disappear quickly because of the hyenas. All he had to do was employ the same method here....

'The idea occurred to him quite naturally, having often imported wild animals. He brought back three hyenas from Africa and transported them from Marseille to the castle in a lorry he drove himself. He hid them in a courtyard in the rear part of the castle where no one could hear them because of the thickness of the walls. Nobody knew of their existence except Baptiste, whom my uncle could rely on completely. Isn't that so, Baptiste?'

'Yes, monsieur. It was I who fed them through an arrow slit. I went every day by bicycle to Versailles to buy the meat, so the cook wouldn't suspect anything.'

'The Carlovitches arrived,' continued Aranc. 'At first my uncle tried to separate the wife from the husband, so as to avoid the need for a crime. She, naturally, refused because she still loved Carlovitch. The situation suited her because it placed my uncle in a position of ridicule.

'She pretended to fear her husband's vengeance, not realising that, in so doing, she was signing his death warrant. She nevertheless gave herself to Saint-Luce with the full consent of Carlovitch, who was desperate to escape their misery.

'That was the state of affairs when M. Herry suddenly arrived at the castle, where nobody desired his presence. He could be a highly inconvenient witness to any crime. My uncle's first reaction was to get him to leave immediately, which is why he received him so coldly.

'But while they were talking, Saint-Luce realised such an attitude would be stupid. Should there be an investigation following the disappearance of Carlovitch, Pierre Herry would be a witness and there would be astonishment and suspicion that Saint-Luce had virtually shown the door to such an old friend—and one who had saved his life. It would be much better to have him stay overnight, which is why my uncle suddenly displayed such cordiality.

'He had not anticipated that M. Herry was blessed with such an extraordinary sense of hearing and would be able to detect, during the night, the howling of the hyenas at the opposite end of the castle. And they had good reason to howl, for they had not been fed for twenty-four hours and you can guess why!'

'Ugh! What a hideous reminder,' interjected Pierre Herry. 'Even more so, now that I understand... That same night, incidentally, I noticed something else, someone used the corridor to go from one room to another.'

'Sonia, probably,' replied Aranc. 'She was going to Saint-Luce's room, or coming back, pretending to hide from her husband.

'The next day, monsieur, you spoke to my uncle about the mysterious howls you'd heard during the night... You noticed his reaction.'

'Of course. He went as white as a sheet.'

'If ever you were to reveal what you'd heard, or bear witness to that effect during an investigation, people might suspect the truth. So you, too, would have to die. He insisted, you will recall, that you stay another night.'

'I remember it well.'

'That was the night you and Carlovitch were both going to die. Sonia was getting restless and talking of leaving. Saint-Luce had to act quickly.

'He started by luring Carlovitch into the library, ostensibly to talk about a job. He caught him by surprise and killed him with a blow from the massive club. Then he carried the body to the hyenas, who hadn't eaten for two days.

'Next, it was to be your turn. He expected to find you asleep, having put a sleeping draught in your glass during dinner. Luckily for you, you woke up and fought with him... Once you'd escaped his trap, he feared you would use your revolver and so he fled.'

'Why didn't he use a revolver instead of that club?' asked Pierre Herry.

'Because of Sonia, who might have heard the shot and come running. He still wasn't sure of her feelings and didn't want to reveal his crimes to her. He was planning to accuse Carlovitch of your murder, then pretend to be attacked himself afterwards. The engineer's disappearance would be taken for someone fleeing a crime, and that damning assumption would mean that nobody would look elsewhere for him. Saint-Luce would have passed it off as a *crise de jalousie.*

'But because of your resistance, he was forced to change his plan, at least in one respect.

'He went back to his room, wounded himself, and cried out for help. Carlovitch was still the suspect. In other words, it was the original plan, with the slight difference that you were now a witness as well as a victim.'

'Thank you for the "slight difference,"' said Herry wryly.

'To my uncle, believe me, it was slight. You've already deduced, I assume, that it was my uncle himself who placed that large block of stone under the portcullis before it was lowered, to prevent it descending all the way. He had to justify her husband's flight to Sonia. He also released the bolts on the park gate and was very satisfied when you went yourself to verify.

'In that way, you served as an impartial witness in Sonia's eyes. Believe me, my uncle asked nothing more of you.'

'Meaning?'

'Meaning he couldn't afford to have you testify in front of a judge, because you would have spoken about the mysterious howls, which he didn't want at any price. So he asked you to stay another night, during which—believe me—you would have disappeared like Carlovitch, and in the same way.

'Your sister's accident saved you miraculously.

'That night again and the following day, Saint-Luce left the hyenas with the corpse. They needed all of two days, driven by hunger, to grind the bones down. The following night he let them loose...'

'They must have gone past the farm,' declared Pierre Herry, 'because Père Antoine heard them howling and his dog went wild.'

'In any case, they finished up in the forest of Meudon, where they were killed shortly afterwards without anyone making a connection.

'That night Saint-Luce finished grinding what was left of the bones and the next day he went out on the moors to scatter the remaining fragments.

'It was a good thing that he had acted so quickly, for the same day

160

the anonymous letter arrived in the Public Prosecutor's office.'

'Who sent it?' asked M. Cordani.

'Why, Sonia, of course. She suspected something. It was Père Antoine who took the letter to Versailles. There was no risk, because he can't read.

'The police didn't find anything, for good reason. The dogs tried to follow the scent of the hyenas, but they were held back.

'Sonia, out of fear for Saint-Luce, didn't dare tell M. Cordani about her suspicions. Quite the opposite: she pretended to believe in Carlovitch's flight.

'Then, when the extensive search drew a blank, she started to accept that her husband had left of his own accord. Having nowhere else to go, and without a *sou*, she agreed to stay with Saint-Luce. But, fearful of Carlovitch's revenge, she refused to leave the castle.'

*****

'That, messieurs, is the first part of the story. There wouldn't have been a second part if my uncle, overconfident, hadn't revealed everything to Sonia one day last year.

'You cannot imagine to what degree that woman is capable of hate and love at the same time. She adored her husband to the same degree she detested Saint-Luce.

'She thought about killing him straight away. But that wasn't sufficient revenge: she preferred a slow agony, a veritable torture through fear. Saint-Luce had once accused her husband of cowardice; she would inflict the same humiliation on him.

'Sonia, also, was a coward in certain respects: she didn't want to be arrested, fearing prison, to which she had a physical revulsion, and which she dreaded more than death.

'It was around that time that I met her. You've all seen it, messieurs. You all know what great powers of seduction she possesses. I've been a victim, just like my uncle...and you M. Herry, not to mention Père Antoine himself. I consented to everything and we organised the plan together....

'There were two elements from my uncle's past which could be used to terrify him: the theft of the miraculous statue and the corpse of Carlovitch devoured by hyenas. We decided to combine those two

161

elements.

'Sonia had two objectives, as I explained. The first was to kill Saint-Luce after a long period of mental agony. The second was to distance herself from his murder by attributing the crime to external forces.

'So it was that I started sending anonymous letters demanding the return of the statue, while at the same time Sonia caused it to disappear.

'Saint-Luce had complete confidence in his mistress, because she had a gift for subterfuge no Frenchwoman possessed. He also, with good reason in that case, believed in Baptiste's loyalty. The cook was of no importance. The disappearance of the statuette took on a mysterious, menacing quality which affected my uncle greatly.

'You know perhaps, Monsieur Herry, that he possessed no moral courage?'

'I'd noticed that often and told M. Allou about it.'

'And then,' continued Aranc, 'I introduced the howling beast. It was a reminder of the Carlovitch escapade. It was I who went to the park walls one night to imitate the cry of the hyena, which I had often heard in Africa. In addition to the terrifying effect Sonia had hoped for, it suggested an outside presence for the murder, with Père Antoine as witness.

'The following day, a new surprise lies in store for us. My uncle has heard of your return, M. Herry, and wants to enlist your aid.

'Although we are taken aback at first, we decide your presence will be an additional guarantee of our safety and Sonia herself insists Saint-Luce goes to find you.

'Saint-Luce will no longer be murdered. We will simulate a suicide, *to which you will be a witness!*

'We concocted the new plan just before my uncle brought you back to the castle. I knew he'd gone to fetch you and I timed my arrival, you will recall, a few hours before yours.

'To make sure you stayed in the castle, I went rapidly back to Versailles to expedite the threatening letter you received the following day. I'd heard about your character from my uncle and so I knew that the best way to make you stay was to order you to leave.

'Besides, Sonia said she would make sure you stayed next to her.

'But to make the suicide plausible in your eyes, we had to keep the

162

deception going, in order to worsen the nervous depression of the victim.

'That's why, on the night of your arrival, I extinguished the candles in the corridor and banged a door.

'Then, late the following afternoon, using the paw of a hyena—I have quite a few in my collection, as you can imagine—I created the beast's footprint which intrigued you so much. I knew you wouldn't notice it that day, being in an out-of-the-way corner, but Baptiste would see it when he swept the corridor the next morning.

'I didn't create it at night because I couldn't risk going into the corridor at night, with everybody watchful because of the extinguished lights of the night before. Besides, Sonia had warned me her lover had no intention of sleeping.

'The trick worked to perfection. I derived great amusement the next day from your theories.

'But I had to leave. I'd announced that the beast would howl three times, so I would have to come back two more nights, and for that I had to be outside the castle.

'The most plausible way to leave was to get myself thrown out. You watched it happen, so I won't spend time describing it.

'I came back that same night and howled again in the shelter of the park walls.'

'Did you come by motor car?' asked M. Cordani.

'I'm not that stupid. Someone would have heard me. I left the vehicle several kilometres away and continued by bicycle, just like the first time.'

'The first time?' interjected Pierre Herry.

'Yes, the day before your arrival.'

'But Saint-Luce told me he'd been hearing the howling for the last four years!'

'Just as he told you previously that he'd been hearing them for two months. He couldn't afford for you to make the connection between the howling and the disappearance of Carlovitch, and that's why he lied to you.

'Sonia had decided the murder would take place the following night. Saint-Luce couldn't be allowed the time to recover. In order to believe the suicide, M. Herry had to see him at the end of his tether.

'You're well aware of the illusion we were trying to create. There

163

would be a threat from the outside in the form of revenge from the Hindus for the theft of the statuette. And Saint-Luce, out of his mind, faced with an imminent and horrible death—as he imagined—would prefer suicide. Everyone would swear to that in good faith: Baptiste, Herry, the cook and the shepherd.

'The next day Sonia made the final preparations. She used her power over poor Père Antoine to ask for his help to escape. What she actually wanted was for him to throw a stone against her shutter.'

'Why?' asked M. Cordani.

'Because she expected everyone would be locked inside the library and she needed to find a way to get one or two of them out of there to witness what happened.

'In Baptiste's case, it would be easy. She would implore her lover, during the day, to spare the poor man who was incapable of defending himself and of providing any useful help. If need be, she would play on his self-respect. As you know, she succeeded. Saint-Luce sent Baptiste away that night.

'In M. Herry's case, it wasn't so simple. But the stratagem was ingenious. Thanks to the shepherd, there would be a metallic noise in the room next to the library. Sonia took it upon herself, by the way she looked at him, to oblige Pierre Herry to go out and confront the intruder. And, as you know, she succeeded in that, too.

'And the stone against the shutters also served another purpose. Indicating the imminence of danger, the noise explained Saint-Luce's sudden terror and his resulting suicide.

'I won't dwell on the statuette, which Sonia put back in its place in the late afternoon to reinforce the moral depression of her lover.

'As for me, my role was simply to imitate the howling beast for the third and last time. I had a well-prepared plan to create a solid alibi for myself.

'I went to the theatre that evening, where I knew I could count on meeting a few friends, to whom I showed myself. In the middle of the last act I slipped away in my motor car and was under the walls of the park by a quarter to twelve. I was planning to return immediately to Paris and join my friends at a bar—pretending that I'd missed them at the end of the show—then going back to Versailles and getting myself arrested by the police, so as to be locked up in a cell at the time of the murder.

'But a dog which suddenly attacked me by the walls changed my plans somewhat. The animal, which I hadn't heard coming (it was mute), jumped on me suddenly and gave me a vicious bite in the arm. Luckily I'd brought a bronze knuckle duster with me and I knocked the animal out.

'But afterwards I had to return to my residence rather than go to Paris. Not only did I need to bandage my hand, which was bleeding profusely, but I had to change my suit because my jacket had been ripped apart.

'What happened at the castle after that? I haven't yet understood.

'But, as you can see, messieurs, I didn't kill anyone!'

*****

Gustave Aranc sat down, completely exhausted.

'What happened at the castle after that?' asked M. Allou. 'It's quite simple....

'As soon as Pierre Herry leaves the library, Sonia shoots her lover who, no doubt, is expecting it and flings himself backwards. I assume that's what happened because Sonia must have known that, to simulate a suicide, the shot has to be fired very close to the body.

'Saint-Luce falls to the floor. But, in order to complete the illusion, the weapon which fired the shot has to be placed in his hand in order for the forensic staff to confirm it was indeed suicide. But Sonia doesn't have time because Herry, whom she had thought to be farther away, has returned almost immediately.

'How to get him out of the room for a second time?

'Baptiste arrives just in time. Whilst Herry is talking to him, his back is towards Sonia. Once Baptiste heads back downstairs, Sonia points to the bedroom door. Herry assumes the murderer must have escaped from the library whilst his back was turned, so he returns to the bedroom once again.

'Sonia switches the weapons. But—as we learnt from the medical examiner—Saint-Luce isn't dead yet. He regains consciousness just long enough to take his revenge. The bullet, fired from the revolver which has just been switched with his—and which was used to shoot him—strikes Sonia in the temple and kills her outright.

165

'You know the rest from Baptiste's confession. Running upstairs at the sound of the second shot, he sees Pierre Herry crouching behind one of the armchairs in the library and opens fire on him, wounding him. Later, when he finds himself alone in the library, he takes the precaution of removing from his master's hand the gun which he believes has not been fired (but which has, on the contrary, been used to kill the two victims.)

'He replaces it with his own, which has just wounded Herry.

'Then, seized by a new fear, he throws the revolver which has been used in both crimes into the moat.

'And that's it, messieurs.'

'But,' asked M. Cordani, 'what made you think Pierre Herry might be innocent when everything pointed to his guilt?'

'First of all, because his deposition cleared Baptiste of all suspicion. A guilty person wouldn't have done that; he would have tried to put the blame on the servant. Similarly, his offended reaction when I offered him an escape route by pretending to believe he could have helped the culprit to escape out of fear.

'Eliminating Pierre Herry left only one solution possible: the correct one. By scouring the minor news items from that period, I discovered the hyena hunt of four years ago. That explained the disappearance of Carlovitch's corpse and provided me, at the same time, with a motive for Saint-Luce's death: Sonia's revenge.

'After that, you've been present when I questioned witnesses, always following my theory of a crime of vengeance. If I suspected the shepherd of having thrown the stone, it was because Sonia had spoken to him that morning and there was no other solution possible, Aranc being in prison when it happened.

'And I deduced the part Aranc had played by the care with which he had constructed an alibi for the time of the crime.'

'Bring in the gendarmes,' ordered M. Cordani.

THE END

166

APPENDIX 1

THE FRENCH LEGAL/POLICE SYSTEM

In the British and American systems, the police and prosecution gather information likely to convict the suspect. The defence gathers information likely to acquit the defendant. Arguments between the two, and the examination of witnesses, are conducted in open court, and refereed by a judge. The winner is decided, in most important cases, by a jury of ordinary citizens.

In the French system, also adopted in many other continental countries, all criminal cases are investigated by an examining magistrate. He or she is a jurist independent of the government and the prosecution service, and is given total authority over a case: from investigating crime scenes; to questioning witnesses; to ordering the arrest of suspects; to preparing the prosecution's case, if any. Much of the "trial" of the evidence goes on in secret during the investigation (confrontations between witnesses; recreations of the crime) working with the police. The final report of the investigating magistrate is supposed to contain all the evidence favourable to both defence and prosecution.

Investigations are frequently long—two years is normal in straightforward cases—but trials are mostly short. Witnesses are called and the evidence is rehearsed in court, but lengthy cross-examination in the British/American style is rare. In the *Cours d'Assises,* which hear serious criminal cases, there are nine jurors, who sit with three professional judges: other criminal cases and appeals are heard by panels of judges alone.

In France, as in Britain, the defendant is theoretically innocent until proven guilty. But in practice there is a strong presumption of guilt if an examining magistrate, having weighed the evidence from both sides over a period of several years, sends a party to court. There is no right of *habeas corpus* in France. Examining magistrates have a right (within limits) to imprison suspects for lengthy periods without trial.

Much of the leg-work during an investigation is done by the police (in towns) or *gendarmerie* (in rural areas), but relations between magistrates and police are not always as good as depicted here. Not only did anyone below the equivalent of Chief Inspector have to defer to the examining magistrate but in the 1930's they also had to cope with the Brigade Mobile—the equivalent of Scotland Yard's Flying Squad, but on a national scale—which could swoop down and usurp their powers without warning. Not surprisingly, their morale was terrible.

There are other differences between police and *gendarmes*. The police (called *Police Nationale* since 1966; before that it was known as the *Surete)* are under the control of the Ministry of the Interior and are considered to be a civilian force. The *Gendarmerie Nationale* is under the control of the Ministry of Defence since Napoleonic days and is considered to be a military force. In addition to policing smaller towns and rural areas, it guards military installations, airports and shipping ports.

Under French law, you cannot disinherit certain heirs *(les parts reserves)*, which you can under Anglo-Saxon law.

APPENDIX 2

VINDRY ON THE DETECTIVE NOVEL

1. 'Le Roman Policier.' Article in Marianne, 26 July 1933

There is much talk at the moment about the detective novel; a little too much. Some praise it to the skies: and when they let go it will crash. Others relegate it to the basement: it will become covered with mould and quickly rot.

Can't we allocate it its just place? Not too high, so as not to make promises it is unable to keep, and avoid disappointment. Not too low, so as to avoid a sense of unremitting decline and the abandonment of all quality.

But in order to be fair about it, we have to recognise what it is. So many judgments have been made about it that, in reality, have nothing to do with it.

The "Detective Novel"! Under this perhaps badly-chosen heading have been lumped totally disparate works; works not without merit, certainly, but not destined for the same public and therefore sowing fateful confusion.

As with the Christmas cracker, everyone was hoping for something else and curses their luck.

Under this heading, adventure novels have been published and called detective novels on the pretext they feature criminals.

The adventure novel is about chance, the unpredictable, fantasy science and the last-minute revelation which upsets all calculations.

The detective novel is rigour, logic, real science and a solution relentlessly deduced from the given facts.

Two genres more different it is impossible to imagine.

The adventure novel is a treasure in a labyrinth; one finds it by chance after a thousand surprising detours. The detective novel is a treasure in a strong-box; one opens the door very simply with a tiny, necessary and sufficient key.

The former must present the complexity of a panorama; the other that of an architectural drawing.

The detective novel must be constructed like a mathematical

169

problem; at a certain point, which is emphasised, all the clues have been provided fairly; and the rigorous solution will become evident to the astute reader.

No, the presence of a criminal is not enough to turn an adventure novel into a detective novel.

Conan Doyle and Gaston Leroux, in several works, were the masters of the detective novel; Wallace, that of the adventure novel.

Something else as well, delivered under the same heading: the police novel.

It includes shoot-outs, rooftop chases, opium dens, made-up detectives and cries of horror.

The detective novel, on the contrary, economises on revolvers and the police chases of pre-war films.

It lets you into the dining-room, with the meal already prepared, and not into the kitchens.

It is not a work of realism or a documentary; it is constructed for the mind. The logic is unreal, or rather, surreal. The master of fact and not its slave.

One cannot accuse it of an "unhealthy influence on youth," for it interests only the intelligence.

So we have three essentially distinct genres:

The adventure novel, about the life of the criminal.

The police novel, about the arrest of the criminal.

The detective novel, about the discovery of the criminal.

And even, dare I say, "discovery" pure and simple: for the criminal and the police are mere accessory elements to the detective novel. Its essence is a mysterious fact which has to be explained naturally; the criminal hides his activities and the detective tries to discover them; their conflicts provide convenient situations: the "givens" of the problem. That's it.

True detective novels are only "police novels" by accident. Maybe we should change the name.

I propose: "Puzzle novel." (1)

Does this confusion between the detective novel, the adventure novel and the police novel result solely from a badly-chosen term?

No: all three possess a common element of fascinating importance: action. Overwhelmed by the speed, one no longer notices the body moving.

(1) *Roman probleme:* "problem novel," or "puzzle novel" (less confusing).

Action dazzles the reader. Alas, it sometimes dazzles the author: of what use is style if the intrigue is enough to excite passion? Superfluous dressing which can only slow down the chase.

Style, however, is not a gilded ornament to be taken out of the wardrobe on festive occasions; it must be true to itself to the end. An umbrella has its own style if it remains perfectly umbrella.

The detective novel has a right to its own style, just like everything else. It can demand its own language, for it stutters in the others.

Its phrasing must be unadorned, the better to fly with the action.

Its narrative must contain everything necessary, but nothing more.

The detective novel, as opposed to the psychological one, does not see the interior but only the exterior. "States of mind" are prohibited, because the culprit must remain hidden.

It's only necessary to reveal what can be seen *immediately* in the action; but to do it properly, by which I mean rigorously; look for the aspect which has impressed the spectator to the crime.

"The cry of horror" is a bit vague. And generally inaccurate: gendarmes very seldom let out cries of horror; and the civil police scarcely more.

No, a detective novel isn't necessarily "badly-written."

It can, incidentally, possess other qualities; one only needs to read the marvellous "atmospheres" of Simenon, who has imposed his intensely personal touch on the genre.

But I've only tried here to bring out the salient aspects of the detective novel or, if you will allow me, the "puzzle novel":

An action;

An equation;

A style.

Perhaps it will then be easier to assign it its proper place.

No, it's not very high: it doesn't lift the spirit in any way; it's a sort of crossword: a simple game of intelligence.

No, it's not very low; it seeks to tap into our need for logic and our faculties of deduction. There's nothing shameful about that.

It's an honest and respectable genre: nothing grandiose and nothing unhealthy. One can, without shame, experience pleasure or boredom equally well. But it's ridiculous to venerate it or despise it.

It can be the source of works that are bad, mediocre or good: and even brilliant if they are signed by Edgar Poe—but they contain a "special something," it's true; even so it's important to acknowledge that Edgar Poe used this mould in which to pour his "precious metal."

2. Extract from a 1941 Radio Francaise broadcast

"Why did I give up the detective novel? For no particular reason: the way one gives up a game one no longer finds amusing. Because the detective novel is nothing more than a game; nothing more and nothing less. Like chess and crossword-puzzles, it has its rules, which constitute its honesty and dignity. I tried my best to play by them and was only interested in the logic: in the problem properly posed and correctly answered."

"In the puzzle?"

"Yes, in the puzzle. Much more so than in the drama or the adventure. I wanted to excite the reader's intellect more than his passion. I don't regret in any way having written detective novels. It was a game where I didn't cheat. If I stopped writing them it's because the game had ceased to amuse me, and one shouldn't write when one doesn't feel like it."

"Can you identify the reason for this change of heart? Or does it remain obscure, even to you?"

"I think I understand. It's gruelling work, but with moments of sheer pleasure and more fascinating than any other game. But now that I'm writing real novels—."

"Les Canjuers, La Cordee, and last year La Haute Neige?"

"Yes, since then I no longer play with my characters, I collaborate with them and I live with them. It's a solemn joy, far from amusement."

3. Extract from Letter to Maurice Renault, editor of "Mystere-Magazine" October 26, 1952

What's the oldest French detective novel? I believe it's Voltaire's "Zadig." A short novel, but rather too long to be a short story.

It conforms to what I believe to be the definition of the genre: "A mystery drama emphasizing logic."

So, three elements:
1. A drama, the part with the action
2. A mystery, the poetic part
3. The logic, the intelligent part

They are terribly difficult to keep in equilibrium. If drama dominates we fall into melodrama or worse, as everyone knows; if mystery dominates, we finish up with a fairy tale, something altogether different which doesn't obey the same laws of credibility; if logic dominates the work degenerates into a game, a chess problem or a crossword and it's no longer a novel.

A great example of equilibrium? "The Mystery of the Yellow Room."